THE LEGEND

OF

TURTLE POND

The Initiation of Tabitha O'Brien

by

MILA A. BALLENTINE

PUBLISHER'S NOTE

This novel is a work of fiction told from the perspective of
fictitious character experiences. The names, places, and
characters are products of the author's imagination. Any
resemblance to actual persons living or dead, business
establishments, event or locals is coincidental.

For

S. J. Dennery

Benjamin Yon Floyd

and

Genevieve Scholl

1

In the distance, the hair of a goddess fastened to the prow of the four-masted ship flowed against the pine in rhythmic waves, eyes nonchalantly staring at the heavens as she led the way and docked at Ládonia's pier alongside scores of passengers lining up on the wharf to board her. Meanwhile, travel chests stood out above the gathering as they punctuated heads in the crowd while others carried their possessions in leather suitcases onto the narrow gangway, entered the lower level, and disappeared into the hull, passing buckets of sand that lined the narrow quarters.

Shortly after boarding the Lavinia, they set sail on a voyage that would be the first for many. There was a familiar look in their eyes, embracing the journey ahead; and yet as they peered through the portholes and got the last glimpses of their loved ones, the coastline diminished behind them leaving much to be desired. And when their attentions waned, their eyes traveled around the confines of the small room and honed in on a beautiful, but otherwise gloomy, dark-haired woman traveling with her family. In no time, their attention turned meddlesome and soon whispers stirred and guileful stares surfaced that concentrated on her archaic, sanguine eyes, fueling misguided notions, rallying ignorance that prompted them to segregate themselves from the trio and yet, their eyes stayed on the O'Briens. The glares were unsettling in and of itself, but she was used to it; she'd been experiencing such glares since childhood.

With all that the family was going through, their intolerance was the last thing she needed, seeing that only a day prior, they had received word concerning their eldest son, Uri. Three weeks earlier, he had boarded the *Genesis,* but halfway through the journey, they encountered a squall out at sea that sunk the vessel five miles off the coast of *Astonia.* This wasn't the way things were supposed to go; their beloved son should be there waiting to receive them. With the

5

weight of her grief upon her, Tabitha rested her head in her husband's arms and wept. Meanwhile, Marc passed his hand along her dark brown mane while his empty stare focused on their eleven-year-old son, Jon sleeping on a cot near them.

Nearing the end of the first day, her guttural wails of grief filled the cabin even as hunger skulked in their stomachs, a primal call beckoned by the aroma of food. Soon afterward, the cook's assistant laid baskets on tables suspended from the ceiling by ropes, a table they gathered at and feasted on vermin-infested bread, their stomachs all too eager to digest it even though its cringe worthy contents soured their bellies and ultimately the journey.

While they ate bitter bread, the hidden delicacies of the upper levels entered their quarters—delectable aromas of stewed meats and potatoes seeped through the floorboards along with the echoes of glasses meeting in a toast, and cheerful chatter. Luckily, out of habit, the O'Briens had brought along green pigeon peas to eat; it sustained them and minimized their exposure to the ship's tainted steerage food.

For most of the journey, when they weren't consuming or sleeping, the passengers gazed through the openings longing for the horizon even as high tides obstructed their view. The temperamental waves either kept them awake or lulled them to sleep, a constant sway that riled their innards. A symptom that progressed to bile spilling from their lips to the floorboards, progressing to a stench that lingered on the wood. From then on, their comfort diminished, their idle time was spent tallying the days left but there were more days than they could fathom before their journey would end.

2

After countless hours of standing in the *crow's nest* above the mast, a crewmember saw a line of green sitting just above the water's edge in the distance.

"Land ho!" he bellowed while a flock of seagulls rode the wind some distance ahead, squawking as they led the *Lavinia ashore*.

The ship entered one of the many waterways surrounding *Astonia* and in no time they docked in *Vermouthshire* – the largest of the three islands, the first port of call. This was where first and second-class passengers got off, and strolled toward the downtown area, aptly lined with specialty shops, catering to the needs of its well-to-do residents. Their elaborate horse-drawn carriages and Model T's parked out front was a constant reminder of their status. Leaving port, the Lavinia passed *Aerona*, the smallest of the three islands – a pier-less, solitudinous island with desolate terrain which lied on the southernmost tip of Vermouthshire.

Soon after, the Lavinia moored in Draíocht Dol, an underdeveloped splendor with rich soil and for the first time in two weeks, passengers from below surfaced visibly emaciated, eyes squinting, reeking of sweat as they welcomed the sun. In their eyes, Astonia was grander than they had ever imagined. The O'Briens were amongst those who emerged from the lower deck but there were passengers in steerage that weren't so lucky. Those who did not make it were buried at sea. Nevertheless, they were survivors of the turbulent voyage; they traveled the narrow walkway leading to the pier and filtered through the small group of passengers who came off the ship ahead of them.

"Keep your head down," Marc whispered as they approached a line of wagons where the drivers offered to carry goods or passengers for a price and lessened the distance between them.

"Look—Dad," Jon pointed to the other end. "Shops! Can we go? Can we, Dad?"

"No, Jon. We don't have time for that right now."

Meanwhile, Tabitha lowered her head, while Jon circled. She grabbed his hand and brought him to her side. A driver perched on high spotted the top of Tabitha's bonnet and tipped his dusty old hat at her as he looked down from the seat of the wagon. Meanwhile, Jon creased his brow as he peered up at a man in a long-sleeved shirt with slacks worn out at the knee, and mud-covered boots. Looking into the man's deep set eyes, and at his unkempt hair sticking out from behind his ears like stuffed straw certainly caused pause.

Marc went over to him swatting gnats along the way. "Can you take us to the other side of the island, close to the river's edge?" he asked.

"I can do that, come."

Marc helped Tabitha and Jon into the back of the wagon. The driver's forehead rippled as he observed them. "The lady can sit up front."

Marc helped himself up and sat next to the driver. "She prefers the back."

"Suit yourself." The driver flapped the reins and the horses cantered down the path giving them ample view of the scenic route, passing varied species of trees standing tall alongside proud plants with earthy greens, sunny yellows, and fiery reds, all attempting to outshine the other in the ambiance. The drive went on for hours, while Tabitha and Jon fought to keep their eyes open but Marc remained awake, eyes surveying the landscape.

"Wait a minute! Slow down please."
The driver slowed the horses to a trot giving Marc the opportunity to notice a small clearing up ahead. Eloquent trees stood straight donning an abundance of leaves and yet rays of sunlight shone through, placing soft illumination on the low shrubs near the raised roots of the trees. Marc zoomed in and focused on a clearing just inside the group of vegetation, wide enough to mold into a haven.

11

"I think this is it," Marc said confidently smiling as he looked at his wife and young son. The wagon came to a standstill and the driver helped them unload their belongings.

"Thank you, sir." Marc paid the fare and shook the driver's hand. It was then Tabitha raised her head. At the same time, the driver fixated on her crimson eyes, and as a result, his grip loosened until his hand fell to his side. He backed away and bumped into the frame of the wagon. He spun around, climbed the wagon, and flapped the reins.

"Yah!" he yelled and the horses galloped down the path leaving a cloud of dust behind them.

"I'm sorry," Tabitha's voice cracked. Marc drew her into his arms, consoling her as he planted a soft kiss on her forehead.

"It's okay. It doesn't matter. We've made it." Marc freed her from his embrace and focused on a particular tree. Then, he opened the chest, retrieved his tool, and proceeded to swing the ax.

3

Now, smoke plumed from the tree stumps Marc cut down weeks prior. A smoky haze with embers periodically rising like fireflies as the wind swept through the area. Nearby, Jon stood beside a fleet of buckets of water and looked on as the flames died. They stayed there until the sun lowered into the horizon, setting off a brilliant orange-yellow display in the sky. While focusing on her husband, Tabitha slipped into a daydream glare just as she reached for and held his hand. Her attention quickly waned in the glare of the dimming fire, and it was in that moment that tears streamed down her cheeks while she dwelled on the loss of her eldest son. Marc let go of her hand and reached for a bucket. His family followed suit, and threw water on the stumps and continued to monitor them to be sure the fires were out before they went inside the cabin.

Straightaway, Tabitha went on to prepare dinner and stood in the kitchen stirring the ladle.

When she was through cooking, she shared out cornmeal porridge, a meal that barely touched let alone fill their stomachs.

"May I be excused?" Jon asked.

They looked at him although Tabitha said, "Yes."

Jon grabbed his towel on the way out to the outhouse, entered the shower separated by paneled wood from the latrine and proceeded to bathe. Meanwhile, runoff from his bath drained through a hole the size of a grapefruit in the floorboard.

After filling Marc's glass with water, Tabitha handed it to him. "I'll wash up as soon as Jon's done."

"I'll go when you're through."

Deep in thought, her eyes scanned the cabin's earthy hue. Brown logs ensured that the room held an infinite darkness outside of the light provided by the fireplace, illuminating the house during the stillness of the night. Then, her line of sight traveled along the mixture used to fill the gaps between the logs. The roughness of Marc's

14

hand gently touching the side of her face drew her attention; she kissed the concave of his hand – a hand that was no stranger to hard work.

She went on to gather the dishes, washed them, and put them away. Afterward, Tabitha dried her hands on her apron, removed it and hung it over the back of the chair.

Shortly afterward, Jon entered the cabin and hung his towel on a hook in the corner of the room.

"I'll tuck you in." Jon climbed into the bed; Tabitha pulled the covers up to his shoulder, kissed his forehead and smiled when she looked into those light-blue eyes looking up at her.

"Mom."

"Yes, dear."

"Dad and I have blue eyes but yours are red, why?"

A question she knew would eventually come. She let out a patient breath. "I'm different, Jon; always have been. I'm not sure what determines someone's eye color but I suspect there will come

15

a time when that type of information will be readily available, but one thing is for sure, we all bleed red. It just so happens that my eyes are this color but that's okay. It doesn't make me any less human, just different."

Anyone observing their exchange would think that it was easy to explain it in that way to a child, even as she knew deep down that she couldn't tell him the ever present truth – that she was capable of doing unspeakable things. It was the very reason why they left Ládonia. Once the townsfolk got wind of her abilities, they blamed her for every ill-fated thing that befell the village.

She tickled Jon's chin, "Do my eyes scare you?"

"No," Jon said cheerily and smiled. His grin reminded her of Uri's when he was that age; they had that in common – a warm smile that melted her heart.

She kissed him on the nose, "Good night."

Meanwhile, Marc stood in the background observing them as she sat at the side of Jon's bed.

"I'm on my way out," he said and stepped outside where the whir of night critters buzzed around him and entered the stall. A short time later, he emerged wearing a long shirt gown and set his foot outside into a pool of mud. He shook his head as he walked back to the cabin and entered.

"In the morning remind me to change the direction the water flows out of the bath; there's an issue with the drainage."

"Okay." She kissed him on the way out.

By the time she returned, everyone was asleep. Tabitha turned down the lamp, lit a candle and brought it along, its flame casting a shadow on Jon and Marc's face along the way while they slept. She entered the kitchen, placed the candle on the table, and sat down. Tabitha briefly looked over her shoulder, removed a linked chain with a cone-shaped pendulum from her pocket and held it by the clasp just above a thin board she placed on the table. The inscriptions on it read, 'yes,' 'no,' 'maybe,' and 'ask again.'

"I'm trying to contact Uri O'Brien, son of Marc and Tabitha – and brother of Jon O'Brien," she said as the flame reflected in her carmine-hued eyes. Then, she closed them and allowed her mind to drift into a state of calm before opening them again.

"I'd like to speak with Uri O'Brien," she restated.

Yet, the silence continued to loom in the motionless room—minutes turned to hours while she sat there waiting for a reply. Her head lowered and elevated as the veil of sleep weighed down her eyes until her head eventually lowered to the table as she drifted into a deep sleep.

After numerous hours of resting soundly on the hard surface, the sun filtered through gaps in the wood and reflected on her face. Upon opening her eyes, Tabitha yawned releasing her morning breath with telltale indentations from sleeping on the hard surface on her face. Not long afterward, an unshakable sadness took hold. Uri did not come to her, nor did they meet in her dreams.

Tabitha rose, strolled to the front door and opened it. The fog had finally lifted from their land and in the distance, Marc and Jon stood in the fields laying seeds. All they needed was for nature to work with them and not against them.

4

They spent the next three months planting and nurturing the seeds they implanted in the rich soil, most of which decomposed or was eaten by critters. Not to mention that the lack of rain didn't help. Aside from that, there were plenty of game in the woods, but the animals were not keen on being caught. In spite of this, the O'Briens managed to scavenge a small amount of food but it was never enough to sustain the family of three. As a result, their sunken eyes told of their hunger and their emaciated bodies illustrated unspeakable hardship, but they knew that at times, progress and hardship were kinfolks.

Grief-stricken, eyes welled up to the point that tears began to flow from them as she leaned against the doorframe, and peered out into the front yard. Marc mourned in other ways, although work consumed his time. Whereas Jon found comfort in child's play, at the heel of his parents, but there was no escaping the sorrow of losing a son.

Once evening befell them, the emptiness and bite of hunger kept her awake but even then, Tabitha's heart ached, all while Jon and Marc went to bed as hungry as they had awakened that day, settling into a deep sleep. Tabitha lightly lifted the sheet and slipped out of bed. Eager for deliverance from her grief, she retrieved her instrument from the pocket of her apron, pulled the thin board from behind the bedpost, and entered the kitchen.

While seated at the table, Tabitha concentrated on the task, "I'm trying to communicate with Uri O'Brien, son of Marc and Tabitha, Jon's older brother."

The candle flickered into a smoke as if a brisk air had entered killed the flame, but there wasn't any. Tabitha relit the candle and silenced her mind but also allowed her thoughts to drift.

"Uri O'Brien, please come forward," she said and the pendulum swayed to 'no,' then to 'ask again.'

"I'd like to speak to Uri O'Brien," she echoed.

The pendulum spun tiresomely and then flew out of her hand. She gasped.

"Who's there?" Tabitha spoke with a tremor in her voice.

"*Albert. Albert Knolls.*" His eerie, breathless tone created a sensation that likened to earthworms crawling beneath her skin.

"What do you want?" she asked without letting a second pass.

"I want to help," he replied, the beginnings of a conversation that would continue well into the predawn hours, his words becoming more purposeful as time went on, rallying hope for what was to come.

Accordingly, in the middle of their chat, Tabitha tiptoed to the door, gently removed the latch and went out into the dark, wild woods.

Meanwhile, the sun continued to rise as she traipsed through an area of moist grass. On the upper echelons of the trees sat a mist.

Nearing the end of the arduous journey, Tabitha halted at the stump of a tree and expelled a series of panting breaths. In a small clearing, an uprooted tree's exposed roots stuck out as it lay on its side. She sat on it and wiped cold sweat from her brow and at that moment, a deep chill crept up her spine. Tabitha abruptly spun around and clumsily fell to the floor. Just a few feet from where she landed was the body of a man with an ax lying next to him. A portion of his straw hat was hidden beneath a pile of dry leaves. Not that he had any use for any of it now, but he wore a smock and by the looks of it, tailored gray slacks. His flesh had long leathered, adhering to the bone like dried meat and his clothing sunk around the bones that remained. As a result, what was once his eyes were now hollow windowless sockets with a plethora of deep grooves. Tabitha clenched her eyes, as she imagined the beaks of eager scavengers stabbing his fleshy eyes until they were no more.

'*I want you to walk two miles north,*' Albert had instructed hours earlier, and she did as he said without knowing if he was leading her astray. His statement, 'I want to help,' compelled her to go.

Tabitha scanned the bark of the trees for moss and walked in the direction where it was most abundant. Out of nowhere, to the left, a translucent man emerged and walked through a tree directly in front of her, prompting the fine hairs on her arms to stand straight.

"I came to this island to build a home and start a family. As you can see, it didn't work out like I'd planned."

"What happened to you?" Tabitha asked uneasily.

"At this point, it doesn't matter. What's most important is that I'm here to help," he said pointing to the right of her. "We have seeds and they need planting." After he shared the

24

information with her, his silhouette disbanded but an unsettling feeling remained.

Tabitha got up from the ground, dusted off her frock and walked in the direction that Albert pointed out, searching for anything that made sense. Before long, she came upon two oxen grazing with large leather saddle bags strapped to their backs. By the looks of their rib cages, which were visible beneath their skin, it was clear that they'd endured months without a master's care. She approached one of them and petted its mane. The ox let out a loud breath and nudged its head. Tabitha lifted the flap of one of the large saddlebags and peered inside where she found all kinds of seeds separated in small pouches occupying it. It was odd that the seeds hadn't grown under the elements but it appears that they were well protected. She grabbed ahold of the rope attached to the oxen and led the way back to the cabin.

By the time she returned, Marc was out of bed working outside, but he stopped what he was doing when he saw Tabitha returning with two oxen.

"Morning," Tabitha said while she tied the oxen to a tree.

"What's going on?" Marc's look bordered on confusion.

"They're the new editions to our family."

"We can't afford them, Tabitha."

She placed her hand on the side of his cheek. "There's no cost associated with them. They're a gift." She kissed him. "It's a sin to refuse a blessing."

Her nonchalant attitude was trying his already tested patience. "You left the door open this morning and it so happened that a stray chicken wandered inside the house and made a mess of things." His tone coarsened.

"It's too early in the day to argue." She turned to walk away but then turned around abruptly.

"Did you say a stray chicken?"

"Yes," he replied impatiently. "You could have at least made breakfast before you left."

26

"Ha! What breakfast? We don't have any food left."

Tabitha raised her frock and ran to the house.

Marc swallowed hard and Jon ran from the bushes to where his father stood.

"What's the matter, dad?"

"*Nothing*, your mother, and I are having a discussion. Go and play."

"Where is it?" Tabitha shouted as she reappeared inside the front door.

"I tied a string to its feet. It's at the left end of the house."

"I've never seen anything like it." Marc shook his head and rested his hand on his waist. "If I told anyone that our dinner walked into my house after weeks of evading me, they'd say I was jesting."

5

Later that evening while the O'Briens laid in their beds, the stirrings of many animals communicating accompanied by dragging sounds kept Tabitha up for much of the night. By the second night, she'd had enough. She got out of bed, wrapped a shawl over her thin shift gown, and put on a mop cap before venturing outside. For the most part, she had no business being out there at that time of night, but the noises made it damn near impossible for her to remain in bed. Based on her observation, the commotion appeared to be caused by the oxen they'd secured hours earlier within a gated area. The same oxen that were now dragging the plow behind them as they traipsed across the field. She stood there dumbfounded, not sure of what to make of it but if the oxen wanted to plow the land while they slept, so be it! She went indoors and went to sleep.

Hours later, sunrise opened a love letter to a new day, and Tabitha woke with it; she raised her head and looked over at Marc lacing up his boots at the edge of their bed.

"Good Morning." Tabitha yawned as she sat up beside him and got out of bed.

"I put the kettle on," he said and grabbed his hat on the way out. Tabitha shrugged a dress she reached for moments earlier on over her head.

"Wait for me." She quickly wrapped a shawl around her shoulders and followed him outside.

Marc stood in front of her with his hat in his hand as they both looked out at rows of symmetrical banks that lined the entire field. "What's this?" Marc asked as the wind sifted through his ash-blond hair. Tabitha turned and looked in the direction of the post and rail fence to the far left of the field near the cabin; inside the fencing, the oxen grazed vigorously.

"I have no idea. I was asleep too," she fibbed.

Incidentally, an uncomfortable feeling came over her. "Where's Jon?"

"Wasn't he with you?"

"Actually, he wasn't." Marc gulped. "Jon!" he yelled.

"Jon!" Tabitha called out, both echoing his name as they crisscrossed the land.

Out of nowhere, a blood curdling, screeching echo resonated through the area.

"Marc!" she yelled.

Hearing her call quickened his steps; he followed her voice and ran past the field where the land was still wild and free. In a small clearing ahead, he saw Tabitha on her knees holding Jon's upper body in her arms and ran up to her just as she lowered her ear to Jon's chest. His shallow heartbeat, hot flesh, and ghastly hue gave her cause for concern.

"Is he okay?" he asked, almost out of breath.

"He has a fever."

He took Jon from her arms and brought him back to the cabin with his wife trailing closely behind.

6

Jon lay on the bed as the kettle whistled in the background. Shortly afterward, Tabitha removed the kettle from the fire, put the tea leaves inside, and let it steep. To the right, Marc sat at the table observing his ill son while Tabitha put the cup to Jon's lips and as he sipped, his body temperature gradually returned to normal, but within a few minutes reverted into a feverish state.

A sense of helplessness came over her and a dull ache surfaced in the pit of her stomach. She wrung out a rag taken from the bowl of cool water and patted his forehead and sang him a lullaby.

Oh beloved son
Emerge from the clouds
And shine like the noonday sun—

The prospect of losing another son made her voice crack and she gave way to sobs. Marc rushed to the foot of the bed and held her.

"Keep your wits about you. It's the only way we'll get through this," he said softly, rubbing the pit of her back; although she didn't intend to, she pulled away from him. Marc reluctantly left her and returned to his station at the table. Tabitha wiped Jon's forehead with the rag, passing it along his face and neckline. She removed her shawl, and wrapped it around his head, turban-style, and placed layers of thick blankets up to his neck. Even so, his temperature continued to rise. Tabitha raised him slightly and put a tin cup with cool water to his lips but instead of him drinking it, it ran down the side of his mouth.

"Drink, Jon. Please—"

Tears spilled from her eyes like torrential rain. All of a sudden, Jon's voice filled the room; but strangely, not in his normal vocalization. By the way, *she* was far from visible and yet she whispered in his ear, conjuring him to speak her words hauntingly in a light effeminate tone, "Don't be afraid. I won't harm you," his words painting the air with each utterance. "Let's be a family." Then, he went silent.

She knew that fevers had a way of encouraging madness, but this—this was something entirely different. Tabitha had done her part, now all she could do was wait for him to recover. From that point onward, she sat beside Marc at the table.

He put his hand atop hers and held it. "I'm tired. I'm going to bed." He retired for the night, but his wife had the rest of the evening ahead of her.

From the table, she observed Jon until him until her head slowly lowered to the tabletop. While resting soundly there, her spirit left her body and hovered above Jon's bed. Tabitha made note of his damp skin before passing directly through the wood and continuing out to the field where the hot breath of the oxen clouded the air around their nostrils. Yet again, they were in the field working the land and Tabitha couldn't figure out how they'd gotten out of the secured fence.

Unexpectedly, whispers carried on the staff of the wind led her further inland to where she found the human remains. Just then, Albert walked out of thin air and her essence trembled at the sight of him.

"What do you want?" Tabitha asked the opaque image fading in and out gradually while the wind stirred a pile of leaves.

"I'm sorry about your son."

"How do you know about him?" Her heart raced.

"She meant him no harm."

"What are you talking about? And who is this *she* that you're talking about? And what does she have to do with my son?"

"We wanted children but we never got a chance to follow through with our plans." He removed his hat and walked to her.

"I'm sorry that your plans didn't work out, but what does that have to do with my son?"

"My wife Cora wants to act as a mother figure to him."

Tabitha recalled Jon's conversation in his feverish state. "Absolutely not – not my son!"

Meanwhile, a trace of a woman's hat peeked out from behind a nearby tree and then retreated.

"It's okay, Cora. Come out. I'd like you to meet Mrs. O'Brien."

A dim woman appeared, and floated toward her.

"I'd like to apologize for taking Jon without getting your permission first. I meant him no harm. Unfortunately, we don't feel a variance of temperatures like the living; a deathly chill is our room temperature, so unintentionally, I kept him out here longer than I should've." Cora explained as best she could.

Tabitha didn't expect to, but she understood, and yet her knowing why Jon was out there did not quell her concerns. "What did you do to him?"

"We were working the land. Jon tired so he rested at the base of a tree and I sang to him until he fell asleep on the wet leaves."

Tabitha couldn't believe what she'd just heard. She'd intended for her life in Draíocht Dol to be different from at the turbulent times they'd experienced in Ládonia, but instead, it appeared to be the culmination of something else. Tabitha knew that she attracted peculiarities, and but this was insanity at best.

"Don't be afraid. We only want to help," Albert assured. He held Cora's hand, "You'll need my head." Tabitha stared at him while she tried to make sense of what he'd said, as he ultimately faded into the darkness.

Meanwhile, in their cabin, a mile away, Tabitha opened her eyes, simultaneously retrieving her spirit. Rising from the hardwood table, she woke to Marc's snoring filling the room. She walked over to Jon, stooped down at the side of his bed and touched his forehead. His body felt different; temperature wise, it appeared to be back to normal, causing willful tears to seep from her eyes.

"Mom, you're hurting me." Jon's muffled words traveled above her bosom. She let go of him and unwound the turban from his head.

"How do you feel?"

"I'm good." Jon climbed out of bed, went to the kitchen, poured himself a cup of water and drank until the glass was empty.

Tabitha put her hands on his shoulders. "Jon, I want you to stay with your father. Do you understand?"

"Yes, ma'am."

"Lock the door behind me. I'll be right back."

She went outside and waited until she heard the door latch behind her, raised the hem of her dress and took off running. An hour later, Tabitha stopped at the site where she had stumbled upon Albert's remains and fell to her knees beside him. Her hands trembled as she reached for, gripped, and detached his skull from his spine. She tore a piece of his garment from his chest, wrapped it around the skull, and walked back to the cabin.

Ever since she was a child, Tabitha tried to forget the thoughts that often surfaced in her head and today was no different. It troubled her that she knew what to do with the skull without foreknowledge of how to use it; the same applied to her use of the pendulum that she used to contact Uri. However, unexpectedly Albert came through the thin veil of the dead impacting life.

Wading through a grassy pathway to her destination, Tabitha dwelled on their current dilemma with Albert and his wife. Strangely, somehow she found herself dwelling on simpler – although equally strange times when she was oblivious to her capabilities. For lack of a better word, oblivious until her mother sat her down at the age of twelve to tell her the truth about an unusual evening they experienced twelve years earlier.

A strange cry echoed throughout their village, cries that grew louder each night. On that particular day, just before sunrise, a noise woke the Finley's that prompted them to open their front door. Just outside their sod home in a wide basket, laid a baby with its tiny foot in the air. A dull achy cry followed. They peered down at a baby wrapped in a blanket that stared back at them. The couple had tried unsuccessfully for years to conceive a child of their own only to have on put on their doorstep so they were taken aback. The Finley's brought the child indoors and cared for her like she was their own. It was the child's cries they'd heard all along, but only the Finley's were brave enough to take on the task. Come to find out that their countrymen callously left her because of the state of her eyes. *Therefore, they* moved her from door to door for days.

Concerned for her welfare, the Finley's traveled to a nearby village to consult with a seer. The clairvoyant, naturally smitten by oddities – and Tabitha being one of the rarest she had seen – held her for some time while she awaited a vision. In the meantime, she glanced at the Finley's fondly.

"Your daughter is a being, unlike this world, has ever seen. She was born with an ability that for centuries prior was passed down by strictly by tutelage. Raise her with a good heart so that her gifts do not become a curse." The psychic gave Tabitha back to Mrs. Finley.

"What gifts?" Mrs. Finley asked.

"They will develop as she discovers them—like a toddler learns to walk before they run."

Learning about her beginnings had deeply affected Tabitha and the way in which she matured had left little hope of finding love. So many tears filled her pubescent eyes when she dwelled on the fact that perhaps her abilities would ensure a lonely existence. A sad thought, but life turned out to be much kinder than she'd anticipated. Even in their bleak circumstances, a smile emerged on her tired face but waned shortly thereafter. Not long afterward, Tabitha arrived at their cabin with the skull concealed under her arms and knocked softly on the door.

Jon let her in. Encouragingly, her husband was still asleep.

"Can I go play, mom?"

Tabitha hesitated. "Okay, but play in front of the house."

Jon wasted no time bolting through the door.

Meanwhile, Tabitha looked at the shrouded skull, eager to discover its secrets, but it would have to wait.

7

Amid the obscurity of night, while her family slept, Tabitha went to the kitchen and retrieved her instrument – the wrapped skull she hid earlier – from its hiding place and placed it on the table. She lit a white candle, and set it on the table to the right of the skull and used its flame to light the wick of a black candle, which she placed on the left side of the skull. After silencing her thoughts, Tabitha concentrated on a focal point.

She placed her index finger over the opening of a tiny bottle and turned it on its side, leaving a dab of oil on her index finger. Tabitha placed the bottle on the table and with her index finger; she traced an X on the skull's forehead. She went on to raise the skull to eye level, looking into the hollow holes where there were once eyes. Their combined energies allowed him to seep into her subconscious, and during this time, the power yoked from the skull connected her to the realm beyond the living.

In a guileless, rapturous trance, Tabitha attempted to engage the spirit.

I stare at death even as I question my mortality

Knowing that one day, I too shall die.

Guide me through the realm of the spirits

As we bond for the sake of advancement and building trust.

You vow to serve as a beacon between the

Living and the dead and if you follow through, I shall serve you.

Thy will-will be mine.

Tabitha returned the skull to the center of the candles and as she did so, a chill spread in the room and moments later, his form defined itself. "Albert, I'm glad you're here."

Their sessions became a weekly routine that drew them closer to each other. And during that time, Albert shared a few things with her. More often than Tabitha liked, his wife, Cora would emerge, taking control of Jon's body while he was asleep, causing him to wander with wide

43

eyes. The very thing Tabitha feared was ultimately allowed; Cora acted as a mother figure to Jon. An even bargain Tabitha thought, after all, Albert shared trade secrets with her, information that she readily passed on to her husband who was better suited to handle the task.

As they agreed, the Knolls worked the field while the O'Briens slept and within a two-month period, their crops began to grow in abundance, making hardship a thing of the past. Marveling at the abundance, Tabitha stood at the edge of the field looking out at the endless rows of crops waiting to be harvested and sighed.

"Marc, I think it would be a good idea if we build a shop by the pier. We can sell our crops to the ships that dock there, and with the profits we make, we can purchase more land."

"When did you come up with that idea?"

"Just now." She smirked. "I think we should do it."

He kissed her on the cheek. "I think I will."

Marc stood beside his wife with a grin on his face while he envisioned her idea in his head.

...

It didn't take long for Marc to follow through with his wife's suggestions, and in a month's time, the shop was in working order, selling goods to the ship's crew and their passengers. Soon word of Marc's success spread to Vermouthshire and caught the ear of one of its wealthiest traders, Donovan Kingsley. Kingsley was the owner of a two-story, twelve-room mansion on Clod Hill, which happened to be the peak of the easternmost point of Astonia and from that location they could see *Draíocht Dol* and *Aerona* from the terrace.

Kingsley, a tall lanky man in his 60's, with a full head of graying brown hair and a long beard, stood in front of a bookshelf peering through the window. He slid his hand inside of his vest, and removed a watch attached to his breast pocket and opened the lid. Both intrigued and troubled by Marc's strategies he scratched his chin while asking himself, "How could a simpleton from the bushes of Draíocht Dol be so ambitious and have the know-how to be that successful in such a short time?"

He turned and walked to the coat rack in the corner, and removed a green tailcoat, put it on and looked in the long, gold oblong mirror. Beside it, a pair of pedestals held large ferns spreading like wild branches at each side of the mirror. He walked over and stood in front of the mirror, and placed a top hat on his head. Kingsley fixed his collar, adjusted his beige pantaloons, and tucked the hem into the tasseled loafers.

He went over and sat at his desk in front of the shelves set against scenic tapestries hung on the wall. Thick gold ropes held the sides of the red velvet drapes that adorned the windows, allowing natural light to enter.

His assistant, Bryson knocked before entering the room. "You called for me, sir?"

"I did, have a seat."

The young man hesitated for a moment but then sat across from him. "I'd like you to make arrangements for me to meet with Mr. O'Brien," he said to the tall blond-haired young man with light blue eyes and a quiet demeanor.

"I'll start working on it right away, sir," Bryson said and left the room.

Shortly thereafter, Anton, Mr. Kingsley's guard, entered the study. The tall muscular man with what appeared to be boulders for fists sat in the chair in front of Mr. Kingsley's desk donning a tailored gray suit that fit expertly against his naturally tanned skin. After their lengthy conversation, Anton emerged from the study.

By the time they were through, Bryson had already arranged to have the chauffeur drive them to the pier to catch the next boat to Draíocht Dol. Anton met Bryson out front as the chauffeur came around to the driveway. "I'll be accompanying you." During the ride through the valley, Anton didn't say a word since they'd left the mansion, but once they arrived in town, he made a request.

"Turn left on Lick Liver Drive," he instructed.

The driver looked at him via the rearview mirror. "Are we still going to the pier?"

"Yes, but I'd like to make a quick stop. I won't be long." Anton stared back at the chauffeur without blinking.

The driver made the turn. "A parking spot is available alongside the last building on the right." The car came to a stop in front of the building at the very end of the street where a man dressed in a gray suit sat with his nose perched in the air in the driver's seat atop of an elaborate Hanoverian-drawn carriage. Their car parked behind a line of vehicles along the sidewalk. They observed as passengers entered the carriage; the driver commanded the reins in a manner in which sent the Hanoverians into an eloquent seemingly floating trot.

"I'll be back," Anton said and got out of the car. "Gentlemen, you're welcome to join me if you like." He unbuttoned his coat. "I won't tell if you won't," he said and smirked.

Bryson let out a deep breath, as he looked at his timepiece, "I'll wait here." Meanwhile, Anton entered the business up ahead.

The chauffeur retrieved a men's magazine with semi-nude pictures from the glove compartment and gazed at it as if he was reading a political magazine. Bryson tried not to stare, but it was hard to ignore women sitting on Victorian chairs wearing see-through gowns with the bulbs of their breasts stuck to the fabric. He cleared his throat and looked out the window at the cars passing by. He looked up at the sign molded into the concrete and brick surface of *The Social Nomad* where boisterous laughter trickled out to the streets.

"I think I'll join him." Bryson left the car, walked over to the building.

As Bryson entered, he saw two gold-stained columns that stood opposite of each other in the structure and heard piano music streaming from a phonograph in the background. Varnished wood panel lined the interior walls, along with numerous framed panoramic views of all of the exotic locales the owner visited. Daisy, the barmaid strutted around the room, retrieving empty mugs and kept the glasses filled.

Most would agree that she was the staple to the establishment more so than the liquor. With her skin on display in the softly lit room, Daisy wore a fringe, off-the-shoulder top that accentuated her breasts and was further highlighted by a coffee-colored corset, which slenderized her waistline, and a voluminous green skirt that flowed to her feet. It was an attire that increased her chances of receiving tips. Daisy walked over to a man in a gray suit seated at the bar and placed a tray of empty beer glasses on the counter next to him.

As Anton drank, foam gathered around his upper lip. After he'd emptied the mug, he firmly rested the glass down on the counter. Behind the counter in front of him stood the bartender – a tall, strapping fellow with wavy dark hair, a tall nose and a thick mustache that was curled at the ends. Behind him, a large mirror set against the back wall of the counter that mirrored the patrons at each stage of their inebriation. At the far end of the room, a group of men in top hats and suits congregated around round tables and shared their day's joys and troubles as they drank themselves into oblivion. Another gathering at the left cheered as they culminated a toast and afterward proceeded to drink.

Anton looked over his shoulder as Bryson entered and gestured for the bartender. "A beer for my friend," Anton said to the bartender/owner, Ben.

An hour later, a slender man of a particular age carrying a high belly that hung over his pants with brusque blond hair entered the bar and sat next to Bryson.

"What are you having today, Mr. Finkelsteen?" Ben asked.

"I'll have the house special!" Ben placed the drink in front of him on a coaster. It was customary for Mr. Finkelsteen to have more than one special and once he did, he became chatty. He looked at Bryson as he held his glass in the air and swayed in his direction.

"What are you drinking?" Bryson asked.

"*Fruit Brandy*. You haven't lived until you've had one."

"Oh really?" Bryson gestured for Ben's attention.

"I'll have what he's having."

Ben smiled. "Mr. Finkelsteen you're a good salesman. Here's another special. It's on the house."

"Much obliged, Ben." Mr. Finkelsteen put the glass to his lips and gulped. Shortly thereafter, Ben served Bryson a glass of Fruit Brandy.

He took a sip, "Whoa! This is strong." A succession of coughs followed.

"Don't worry about that, son. It will make you strong." He patted Bryson's back sternly.

Bryson coughed one more time before he gave way to laughter. Ben smiled as he and Mr. Finkelsteen made eye contact and shook his head.

"Don't let the pleasantries fool you. Beware!" Mr. Finkelsteen said as he held his glass up above the counter while periodically spilling his Brandy. Ben eyed him as he adjusted the cuff of his long-sleeved white shirt; he looked sharp in his trademark vest, dress pants, and bow tie. "Mr. Finkelsteen, these people don't want to hear your crazy stories. They are here to drink and have a good time," he said as he dried a glass and put it beneath the shelf.

In his drunken stupor, he pointed at Ben, "They used to call him the gentle giant until he had a dust-up with one of the patrons. One afternoon, a brazen drunk approached Daisy and grabbed her around the waist, knocking a tray of empty glasses out of her hand. Glass shattered everywhere while he rubbed his alcohol enthused sweat onto the pinnacle of her bosom." Once he finished his story, Mr. Finkelsteen let out a wild chuckle.

"Ben ran up to him and beat him senseless. Then, he grabbed him by his breeches and tossed him out of the bar like yesterday's trash." Mr. Finkelsteen stopped only to take another gulp of his drink. "Now we keep it simple and call him Ben; the only thing gentle about that man is the way he mixes his drinks."

Bryson smirked, lifted the glass and drank.

"That's enough, buddy," Ben retrieved the half-empty glass from Mr. Finkelsteen.

"No arguments here buddy," he said, and motioned to step down from the stool but instead tipped it over, sending him toppling backward onto the floor. Anton and Bryson rushed to his aide and helped Mr. Finkelsteen to his feet.

Ben huffed and swayed his hand. "Ah, just lay him down on one of the booth seats in the corner. He'll dry out eventually."

They walked him to the seating area and put him to lie down on the seat.

"Get your paws off me," Mr. Finkelsteen slurred. His belly towered above head level as he laid there, legs hanging off the edge of the seat. Bryson looked on and shook his head while he observed him talking to himself.

"We should go before we end up like him," Bryson said.

"I don't know about you but I can hold my liquor."

"I'm sure you can, but can we go now?" Bryson moved toward the entrance.

Anton sighed and looked at his timepiece. "Alright, I'll go settle the tab and then we'll be on our way out of here." He walked back to the counter. "How much do I owe you?"

"Four dollars. Your friend's bill is twelve."

"I had one drink." Bryson walked over to the bar. "Twelve dollars? It takes me three months to make that kind of money."

"Don't worry about it. I'll take care of it." Anton opened his wallet, flipped through a series of bills, and removed sixteen dollars.

55

"Fortunately for you, I make twice that in a month." He gave him the money. Ben counted them and then put them in the register.

"Mr. Finkelsteen never quite gets around to sharing the price. I wonder why." Ben smirked and went on to tend to the next customer.

By then, Bryson and Anton had left the bar, and walked out to the car. The chauffeur opened the door, and moments later, they drove away from Lick Liver Lane. The stores blurred as the car drove away, and soon the rustling flow of the sea grew louder as they neared the seaport where seabirds flying above communicated with one another as they circled and perched along the wharf. A short time later, the chauffeur parked; they walked to the *Gáleon,* a single-mast vessel, boarded it and set sail for Draíocht Dol.

An hour later, the Gáleon coasted into Draíocht Dol's wharf and a deck hand tied the boat to the pier. Anton got off first and Bryson followed him down the boardwalk that led to the stores along the seaport.

Anton stopped abruptly and held Bryson by the shoulder. "Let me do the talking."

"Mr. Kingsley told me to arrange a meeting," Bryson said sternly. Anton tightened his grip on his shoulder.

"I know, but the situation requires a certain touch. Wait here while I make the necessary arrangements."

"All right." Bryson backed off. He shoved his hands in his pockets, walked to the rocky edge of the pier, took off his boots and walked the shoreline. As the rushing water wet his feet, he cringed. He didn't mind boat rides but never cared for sea bathing. The ocean retreated and rolled up on the sands once more. He backed away from the shore and walked back to the docks. Anton stood with his hands folded waiting for him.

"Are you through with your romantic stroll on the beach?"

Bryson shrugged with a sigh. "Did everything go as planned?"

"It did. He'll meet with Mr. Kingsley by the end of the week."

"That's great. Let's go."

8

The last time Marc saw Vermouthshire was through a porthole on the Lavinia. This time, he stood on deck as the ship left the port; the breath of the ocean washing over him, reminding him of when they'd left Ládonia, three years ago. After some time had passed, the constant motion of the ship made his stomach churn. Luckily, the voyage was short; they docked at the busy port of Vermouthshire within the hour.

Taking in the scenery, he realized that Vermouthshire was nothing like the humble countryside of Draíocht Dol. Marc glanced down at his clean, but tattered clothing and scratched his head. He took the suspenders off his shoulders, tucked his shirt in his pants, and put the straps back in place. He saw the man he spoke with days earlier, some distance ahead leaning against a highly-polished black vehicle and walked to him.

Anton stood with his hands in his pockets. "Good afternoon, Mr. O'Brien."

"Good afternoon."

"Let's get going. Mr. Kingsley is waiting."

He got in the car and it pulled away from the pier.

Driving in an automobile was new to him; he was used to the sway and drag of driving a wagon. He felt a woozy feeling that he likened to seasickness – a feeling that worsened as the driver increased the rate of speed up Clod Hill. He exhaled sharply when the car came to a stop outside Kingsley's mansion.

He wasn't easy to impress, but the sheer size of the light gray house with a large mahogany door and an oval decorative mirror in the center caught his eye. They stepped out of the car, the driver drove away and entered the garage. The duo walked up the steps to the front door and rang the bell. Lenard – the butler, a balding, older man dressed in black answered the door.

"Come in," he said in a dull mutter.

"This way, please," he directed. "Mr. Kingsley's in the study. Wait here while I announce your arrival."

Anton turned to him, "He won't be long." Marc nodded. He looked around the windowless hall and lowered his gaze, to see his reflection on the hardwood floor.

Moments later, Lenard returned. "He'll see you now." He moseyed down the hall, with Marc behind him, opened the door and Marc entered.

"Good afternoon, Mr. Kingsley." Their eyes met. "You sent for me?"

"Yes," he stated while standing in front of a large portrait of himself in an ornate frame hanging directly behind him on the north wall. His eyes traveled the room to see fresh roses resting in vases atop sophisticated accent tables. Thanks to the room's large bay windows, which allowed ample natural light to enter the room, Marc squinted as he extended his hand. At the same time, he noticed a budding rose garden right outside the window. "Good afternoon, Mr.

61

O'Brien," he shook his hand. "I'm glad you could make it. Have a seat. Would you like a drink?" Mr. Kingsley walked over to a modest wet bar at the far end of the room and poured himself a drink.

"No thank you. I don't drink."

Kingsley scoffed, "Men shouldn't discuss business without a stiff drink," he said chillingly.

"Well … since you put it that way, I guess I will have a drink but nothing too strong."

A wide smile graced Kingsley's face. "Attaboy!" Mr. Kingsley poured him a drink before walking around his desk and sitting down.

"You must be wondering why I asked you to come here, so I'll get right to it." He eased back into the chair.

"You've made quite a name for yourself in Draíocht Dol and because of it – I lost a considerable amount of customers. I don't take kindly to competitors of any kind."

Marc stated his case, "I have no control over what your customer's do; if they choose to purchase my produce over yours, it's on them."

"I'm aware of that, Mr. O'Brien. Look, I'm willing to make you a proposal. I'll buy all of your crops *if* you stop selling to the ships that dock at Draíocht Dol. As a matter of fact, I'll continue to buy all of your crops if you go out of business," his expression hardened as he said it.

"Now, before you give me your answer, I'd like you to think about it. Go home and spend time with your family. You can send me your response at the following address." He took out a card and pushed it forward on the desk. Marc took the card and put it in his pocket.

"I hope we can come to an agreement," Kingsley said.

"On the way out, can you tell Anton to see me, please?"

"Sure." Marc put the glass to his lips, emptied it, and gave the glass to him. "Thank you for the drink." They shook hands and he left the room.

Marc passed him as he stood outside the door. "Mr. Kingsley would like to see you."

Anton went into the study while Marc waited in the hallway.

Moments later, Lenard came down the hall. "Is everything all right, sir?"

"Yes. I'm waiting for Anton."

"All right then. If you need anything, I'll be right down the hall."

Soon afterward, Anton came out of the study.

"We should get going … before it gets too dark." They strode down the hall to the exit. By then, the chauffeur had already brought the car out front.

"Let's go. The last boat leaves in an hour," Anton said. They entered and drove to town.

By that time, the pulse of the town had slowed considerably; Marc arrived in the nick of time and caught the last boat to Draíocht Dol. He boarded the ship and set sail, and once he saw the outline of the humble island he called home, he let out a deep breath. The vessel docked at

Draíocht Dol, he got off, climbed their wagon parked near their shop and drove home. By the time he was halfway to his destination dusk was upon him, and before long, he could see their home up ahead. He eased the pace, bringing the horses to a stop at the side of the cabin and stepped down. The cabin's door swung open and Jon ran out to him.

"Do you need help, pa?"

"Not today," he said and hugged him. Jon ran off to the side somewhere.

Tabitha entered the doorway and leaned against the frame. The wind flared the edges of her dark hair as she smiled, eyes lessening within the slopes of her cheeks. Giddy sensations filled his stomach and goose bumps reared their heads. He walked over to her, raised her jawline and kissed her longingly.

"You're beautiful. I love you, dearly," he said. It made him think of times past when they were young and relatively carefree.

During their childhood, he had no choice but to gaze upon her from afar, while she sat on the steps in front of her parent's home. Meanwhile, in the middle of the road in front of her yard, a group of children from the neighborhood jumped over each others crouched backs. She got up to walk over to them. When they saw her approaching, they stopped what they were doing, and picked up stones to pelt at her. She cringed as she saw a succession of rocks coming her way, each inflicting a harmful blow. Instinctively, she shielded her face with her hands. At that moment, Marc stood inside his parent's home by an open window and yelled, "STOP!"

He ran outside and bolted toward them. The gang paused at the sight of his reddening face and balled fist, pumping as he ran swiftly toward them. They dropped their stones and ran off. Consequently, Tabitha crumbled to the floor and wailed. Marc ran over to her.

"Are you okay?" Tabitha raised her head and looked at him; it was the first time he'd seen her

up close and he had been lost in her red eyes ever since.

Luckily, he made her his wife; a deed he never regretted. He ran his index finger along his wife's cheek. "Let's talk," he led her inside the cabin and sat at the table.

"I met with Mr. Kingsley."

Tabitha listened and picked her nails.

"He is interested in buying our crops."

"That sounds promising."

"Not so fast, there's a catch." He paused and looked off to the side.

"He wants me to stop selling to the ships. If I do that I will lose customers."

Tabitha's thoughts drifted into deep plains. She went over to the kitchen counter, grabbed one of the potatoes from the bowl on the counter and started to peel it.

"Don't entertain the thought, Marc, not even for a second! All he wants is to keep you under his shoe."

"Hear me out first … he's interested in buying the entire crop. There's no harm in that." Marc sighed, posture slumping as he sat in the chair.

"But there is, Marc. He will buy it at the lowest price and continue trading his goods at a high price, and you – my love, will become insignificant. There will be no tales to tell of your savvy business maneuvers or your wealth because you won't have a business."

Marc let it all set in. It was clear to him that Tabitha had thought things out more than he had. Shamed, he looked down at the table and drew imaginary symbols on the surface.

"You're right. I won't do it."

Tabitha put the potato aside and wiped her hand on her apron. She went over to him and kissed his forehead. "That's what I wanted to hear." She went back to peeling the potatoes. "We're having potato soup for dinner," Tabitha said while peering out the window.

"My favorite."

She looked over her shoulder at him and smiled. "I know." The room went silent for some time. "You've made the right decision. You're paving the way to have something to pass onto your sons besides your surname." Realizing her slip of the tongue, the knife fell from her hand. She hadn't thought about Uri for some time now and in doing so, she removed a scab that had yet to heal. Tabitha stared off into the distance as tears fell upon her reddening cheeks. *How could I forget him?* Although, she'd never forgot his tender smile. A pillaging sadness came over her that progressed to sobs.

Marc came to her side. "Are you okay?" He turned her to face him and held her.

"We have Jon; he's grown into a handsome young man and someday he'll take over the shop, till the fields and raise his own family on these lands … long after we're gone."

Later on that evening, in the comfort of their cabin, the fireplace illuminated the room. Tabitha stood in the kitchen stirring the pot on the wood

69

stove. When it was finished, she removed it and shared out the food. Moments later, they gathered at the dinner table and ate supper.

"Your soups are delicious," Marc complimented.

"Thank you." She sipped the contents of the spoon.

"Pa, can I go to the pond tomorrow?"

"What pond?" Marc put his spoon beside the bowl.

"It's in the middle of our boundary," Jon said enthusiastically.

"Okay. Yeah, that's right … I do recall seeing it when we first marked our boundary but I don't think that that's a good idea. I don't want you wandering through places that I have yet to explore."

"But I'm fourteen." When last he was there, he was eleven. "I'll be careful," Jon insisted.

"I said no." His son's lip visibly grew an inch. "Tomorrow I'll bring you to the shop. I'm going to teach you how to run the business."

Instantaneously, Jon's disappointment turned to excitement.

♦♦♦

The next morning, Jon woke up earlier than they did, ate breakfast and was ready to go. Marc woke not long afterward and sat at the table eating while Tabitha put the dishes away. Once he'd finished his meal, Marc came up behind her and kissed her on the shoulder.

"We're heading out. I want to get an early start. I'll see you later this afternoon." He put his hat on and left the cabin.

Jon hugged her, "See you later, Ma," and hustled out the door.

An hour later, the horses grazed beneath a broad tree beside the store where Marc parked the wagon and went indoors. Jon brought in the short barrels from the wagon and stacked them on the open crates inside the shop while Marc observed from where he stood behind the counter folding bags. A woman entered their store and walked through the aisles, handling the produce as she went along. She grabbed two apples and sweet potatoes and placed them on the counter.

"Did you find everything you were looking for?" Jon asked while moving toward the register.

"Yes, thank you for asking," She replied and smiled at him.

"That will be twenty-five cents." She opened her coin purse, took out a quarter, and placed it in his hands. He placed her items in a cloth sack and handed her the bag.

"Thank you for doing business with us and please come again." She took her belongings.

"I will," and she was on her way.

"You're doing an excellent job. At this rate, you'll be running the business in no time." Jon's smile eclipsed his cheeks. He looked around the room with stars in his eyes.

"Before I forget, I'd like you to drop this letter in the mailbox inside the general store." Jon took the letter and left the shop. He returned a few minutes later and continued carrying the goods indoors.

"You can finish that later. We got an order while you were gone. Prepare five pounds of corn and five pounds of potatoes, separate please."

Jon wasted no time doing as his father requested.

⁙

With each passing day, Marc enjoyed working side-by-side with his son at the shop, but at home, Tabitha found that her patience was waning. Before then, her days consisted of toiling in the fields, but even during those tiresome moments, she enjoyed the comforts of watching her son grow. However lately, she had been spending much of her days alone. Elation came only when she saw their silhouettes within the eye of the low-lying sun as they ventured home – a joy that heightened as they parked beside her and stepped down.

"How was work today?"

"Productive," he said as they proceeded to remove the barrels from the wagon.

73

"The apple orchard is ready to be harvested. We should pick them before the birds come."

Marc did not respond; they continued to work around her as if she weren't there.

"When will we pick the apples?" she asked.

"I need him for the next few days, but I can spare him on Sunday."

She exhaled deeply. "All right." Tabitha went inside and stirred the pot.

An hour later, Marc entered the kitchen. "What's for dinner?"

"A fresh pot of nothing."

"What does that mean?" he asked with a hand resting on his hip.

"Exactly what I said, nothing."

"Is there something that you'd like to get off your chest?"

She dropped the spoon on the counter; the contents of the pot went on to bubble and pop in the cauldron. "A lot. I don't like being home alone. I'm used to you being gone for half the day, but not Jon. I miss him. I'm not afraid of

74

hard work, but it's hard doing all of it by myself. I'm always exhausted."

He put his arm around her shoulder. "I'm sorry for the stress that these changes have caused, but the boy has to learn how to be a man and he can't do that by hanging onto the tail of your dress."

"He's my *son*!"

"No Tabitha, he's *our* son. It's been a long day. I don't want to argue. We'll work something out. You can have him with you three days out of the week, but I need him at the store. I'm trying to build a legacy to leave behind."

Her anger simmered and lowered all at once. He tried to hug and kissed her, but her arms stayed to her side.

"Just give it a chance. I'm doing this for us. Her head lowered into his chest. Eventually, she raised her arms and consoled him. Afterward, she returned to the kitchen, shared out the vegetable soup and placed the bowls on the table.

That evening, little was said while they ate and instead tentative glances were exchanged. Their bellies were filled, any yet she was discontent. When they were through, Tabitha ushered their bowls away in silence, scraped the remnants in the trash, and stood there for far too long staring at nothing in particular. Marc got up from the table and walked to her.

"Tomorrow, I'm taking you two to the pond. We can carry food and spend a day enjoying each other's company."

"Really?" Tabitha turned to him with the gaze of a freed man.

"Yes, love." He embraced her and put his lips to her ear. "I love you, more than words could say. I'm sorry if I offended you in any way." Her emotions toppled, releasing a storm of tears on his garments. "It's okay, my love." He passed a hand through her hair. "Let's go to bed. We have a long day ahead of us."

The next day, Tabitha woke with an eagerness to cease the day as the sun peaked from behind the hills in the east. The pot was already warming on the wood stove and the air teeming with the aroma of porridge long before Marc and Jon woke. In no time, their mouths covered the spoons and licked them dry.

"We should get ready to leave," Marc said.

She glanced at the tray of meat warming by the fireplace. "Sure. I'm almost done. The meat is already smoked and the bread is warming in the oven as we speak." She hung a fresh batch of dried herbs from a hook on the ceiling. "I'll be ready soon."

They all did their part to prepare for the journey; Jon stocked the wagon while Tabitha removed the bread and let it cool before placing it in a basket, along with the meat she'd wrapped in cheesecloth and wax paper to hold in the moisture. And once they were ready to leave, she put her bonnet on and took the rest of the items to the wagon. Marc grabbed his hat on the way out and closed the door behind him.

"Do we have everything?" He scanned the contents of the wagon.

Tabitha nodded. He helped her up to the seat of the wagon while Jon climbed in the back. Moments later, the horses trotted down the path. It was the first time they'd gone anywhere for leisure since they came to Draíocht Dol so they savored the scenery and the breathtaking fragrance of the trees mixing unapologetically with other – not so pleasant varieties, but the beauty they exuded when they meshed was undeniable.

Within two hours, they came upon the pond and parked the wagon beneath a tree. It sat on the landscape like a large misshapen mirror, reflecting everything around it.

"Is this it?" Tabitha looked over her shoulder at her son.

Jon held on to the base of the driver's seat, came up on his knees and looked out at the surface of the land. "Yes, it is."

Marc tied the horses and left them to graze on the greenery. He lifted Tabitha down from the wagon. Jon jumped down and took out the basket of food. Meanwhile, Tabitha laid the blanket a good distance away from the horses in the shade. Then, she waved for Jon to bring the basket. He brought it over and they joined her on the blanket, broke bread, ate meat, and washed it all down with a glass of freshly squeezed lemonade that Tabitha made earlier. After they'd finished eating, they laid like stuffed pigs on their back, enjoying the breeze as it combed through the land.

Jon was the first to sit up. "Can I swim in the pond?"

"Do you even remember how to swim?" she asked, looking up at him.

"Let him go," Marc said softly to her.

"Go ahead, but be careful."

Before she even said *go,* he took off running, undressing along the way, leaving only his undergarment on and jumped in. They looked on as splashed about, darting his body through the water without a care in the world.

Tabitha laughed, "He's so wild and free."

"Yes, he might as well enjoy his youth. It goes by so fast." Marc looked on in amusement.

Tabitha moved in closer, he held her and pulled her on top of him. She briefly looked out at the pond and returned to his gaze, ultimately losing herself in his blue eyes. Tabitha smiled, "I will remember this day when we're old and gray," she said lowered her head and kissed him.

After they'd wrapped up their outing at the pond, the horse's led them home, their trot resounding as it made contact with the ground. They'd spent most of the day outdoors and now all they wanted to do was sleep. For the most part, Jon got a head start, he laid in the back of the wagon wrapped in the blanket. Tabitha's mood lightened to the point that she couldn't stop smiling, so much so that she didn't focus on scenery during the ride home. She was too busy reliving their day in her head and by the time the horses came to a stop outside their home, the sun dimmed in the background. It was an exhausting day and any energy they had left was spent unloading the wagon, watering the horses and freshening up before going to bed.

•••

A cold chill woke Tabitha and when she opened her eyes, she saw Albert's face directly above hers and it took every ounce of control that she had not to scream. "What do you want? Can't you see that I'm trying to sleep?" she asked while she glared at him. Immediately thereafter, she closed her eyes, but once again, the chill that woke her earlier got colder and her eyes flew open.

"We need to talk," he said, sternly facing her. She got out of bed and retrieved her instruments from their hiding place. Before long, the gleam of the candles reflected in her eyes as she peered at the skull.

81

"We haven't spoken in a while. How's your family?"

"Overall, things are going well. I can't complain. Our business is making a profit and our crops are abundant and healthy."

"I'm glad that you're happy with the way things have turned."

"Why are you here?" she asked.

"You haven't made any offerings in months and yet you continue to reap the fruits of our labor. That coupled with the fact that your son comes home so tired from working all day that his body is non-responsive to Cora's summons. She's not happy about that and neither am I."

Tabitha tried to think of a reason why she failed to follow through with her end of the bargain but found none. "It was out of my control. Marc needed Jon. I've suffered too. I had to do all the work on my own."

"All of the work? Have you forgotten what my wife and I have done?"

"No, not at all. I'm grateful for all that you've done. We couldn't have done all of this without you. Things just got out of hand."

Silence fell between them as she waited for his response. After an hour passed, she called out to him, "Albert—are you there?"

The chill she previously felt left the room and was replaced by a chill deep in her bones. She stayed there until the candles burned out in the hopes that he would return, but he didn't. Eventually, she grew tired of waiting; Tabitha put away her instruments and went back to bed.

She snuggled up to Marc and enjoyed a few hours of sound sleep until a pungent, stifling odor that she recognized made her nose recoil. Tabitha woke wide-eyed and coughing to a smoke-filled room. She sprung out of bed, opened the door, and shook Marc and Jon until they were conscious enough for her to steer them outdoors into the fog of smoke blanketing their land. Within an hour or so, the sky began to lighten.

All they could do was watch and wait until the light of day.

9

By sunrise, the haze faded they it was then that they realized that their land was unscathed, yet an unsettling feeling remained.

"Where did it come from?" Marc asked as he laced up his boots.

"I have no idea. It could've been a brush fire," she added while clearing the dishes from the table.

"Would you be okay with me taking Jon to the shop with me today?"

"Sure. I can manage," Tabitha said and smiled.

He kissed her on the cheek, "In that case, we'll see you later."

Jon took a small bun from the breadbasket, put it in his pocket, hugged her and left shortly after his father. Tabitha stood inside the doorway watching them drive down the path and over the hill.

Once they were out of sight, she went out to the field, shucked corn and stowed them in the wheelbarrow. Afterward, she steered the pushcart to the cabin and filled the short barrels, a task that took three trips to complete in the scorching heat. During that time, she paused when she heard aggressive huff falls coming from below the hill, and dust-clouded figures, which soon became clear. Still early in the day, Tabitha wasn't expecting them back so soon but she wasn't bothered either until she realized the speed in which the horses came into the yard. She quickly moved aside in time to avoid the cloud of dust coming in with them.

They were barely recognizable, their soot-covered faces hinting at something distressing. Tabitha ran to the wagon. "What happened to you two?" she asked anxiously.

"The shop ..." he couldn't bring himself to mutter the words. "Our business ... it—it burned to the ground." Tabitha dropped to her knees in a blank stare.

"All that we've worked so hard to build went up in flames," Marc said, clearly on the verge of tears as he lowered his head.

From that moment onward, they said little to each other and spent the rest of the day dwelling on their loss. They had very little urge to eat and went to bed that evening with much on their mind, and woke the following day with the troubles of the previous day.

A line of sunlight came through a slit between the drapes and rested upon her face. She gathered the strength to get out of bed, lit the fireplace, and stood there for a while staring at the flames.

"We'll get through this," Marc said putting his arms around her waist.

"How?" Tabitha wiped away tears and turned to him.

"The same way we always do – by working together."

He made it seem so easy, but it was hard to start over when they had lost everything within a matter of minutes.

"We still have our crops. We can stock the wagon, park it near where the shop was and continue to sell our goods."

She touched the side of his face. "Can we?"

He kissed her forehead. "Of course, we can."

She rested her chin on his shoulder, which gave her an ample view of the room. "Where's Jon?"

"I haven't the slightest idea, I just woke up not long ago," Marc said, creasing his forehead. "Didn't you see him when you woke up earlier?"

"No—"

Marc opened the front door, looked around the yard and ventured out to the apple fields. Having not found Jon there, he continued onward to the cornfields and found him there shucking corn.

"Jon." He walked up to him.

"Morning, pa."

"We were worried when he couldn't find you."

"I'm fine, pa. I was restless, so I figured that I'd come out here and get a head start."

.•.

Jon hadn't returned and Marc had been gone for a while, so Tabitha ventured further out into the fields. She was relieved to see them working alongside each other, but as she went over to them ready to mince words, she held her tongue as she thought of what Marc said earlier, 'We can do it if we work together.'

"Jon …" she said approaching them, "please let us know the next time you decide to leave that early in the morning, especially after what happened the last time."

"Okay."

"I don't want a repeat of the last incident." She ran her fingers through his light-brown hair and then went to the other end of the row and worked her way toward them.

By noon, they stopped for the day and brought the crops back to the cabin. Tabitha went inside to prepare supper leaving Jon to unpack the corn, put it in short barrels and store them in the shed. Tabitha went inside and stood in the kitchen by the window. Moments later, she heard the vibration of the glass rattling in the pane, stepped outside, and honed in on the familiar sound of the reverberation of horses galloping in the distance. The outline of three men coming down the trail to their home manifested, and a short time later, they entered their yard. One rode in on a horse, while another sat next to the driver. Marc recognized the one sitting next to the driver as Anton removed his hat.

"What brings you out here?" Marc asked,

"Mr. Kingsley received your letter. He wasn't pleased with your reply."

"It's unfortunate that he felt that way, but ultimately it was my decision to make."

Hearing busy chatter outside, Tabitha came to the front door shielding her eye from the gleam of the sun with her hand. Anton came over to Marc and stood between him and Jon.

"Is he your son?" Anton held Jon by the shoulder.

"Yes."

"He's a big boy—practically grown. Are you sure that you wouldn't like more time to reconsider his offer?"

"No. My decision is final."

Tabitha stepped outside. "Marc ... who are they?"

"Mr. Kingsley's men ... they came to discuss my reply to his proposal."

Tabitha sighed and went back to the kitchen.

"I wish that you felt differently," Anton said, his jaw tensing as he forced an object up against Jon's side. He forcefully gripped the back of Jon's neck and put the muzzle of the gun to his side, urging him to move away from Marc. Jon tensed and looked at his father with a terrified look in his eyes.

"Anton—what is going on?" Bryson shouted from atop the horse.

"Don't concern yourself with what I'm doing."

Gill, the other man with them jumped down from the bed of the wagon – pistol in hand and pointed it at Marc. "Don't move."

"Reconsider or else I'll end him," Anton said with a diabolical grimace.

Something didn't seem right, so Tabitha went to the front door.

Upon sight of the spectacle, she called out, "Marc!" and ran toward Jon,

Gill fired a shot at the ground directly in front of her, stopping her in her tracks. "Don't let them hurt our son."

"Don't come any closer," Gill said without little remorse.

"Okay," she said hands apart in the air. "I won't. Just—don't hurt him," fighting tears and the urge to move forward.

"Have you lost your mind, Anton? Stop this madness, now!" Bryson shouted at the tip of his voice.

"You should've listened to me and reconsider your decision," Anton said and pushed the muzzle further into Jon's ribcage. "And you …" he pointed the gun briefly at Bryson, "shut your trap before I shoot you too," he said.

"So what's it going to be? Are you going to agree to Mr. Kingsley terms or not?" Anton tightened his grip on Jon's neck.

Marc swallowed, "My answer is the same and it won't change a month or a year from now."

As the words escaped his mouth, the deafening boom of the pistol firing echoed. An unsettling scream followed that disturbed resting birds sending them to flight. The horse stood on its hind legs, and Bryson was thrown to the ground.

Marc fell to his knees and crawled to Jon on all fours. He held his upper body in his arms and applied pressure to his wound but blood still gushed around his hands. Then, numbness gave way to wails. Tabitha ran toward them and also fell to her knees as she witnessed first hand her son's life fading which heightened her cries. As her cries heightened, Marc sobbed silently and lowered his head all while Anton stood above them smiling.

"I warned you." He put the gun back into the holster under his arm.

Marc came up to a standing position with Jon in his arms, his low cries turning into growing sobs. Grief-stricken, he glared at Anton, turned and carried Jon to the house.

"Hey! I'm not done with you yet." Anton shouted.

Marc continued to walk; Anton sighed, pulled the gun from his side, and pointed it directly at his back. "Stop right there or else I'll shoot."

"Haven't you caused enough harm?" Bryson asked.

Marc continued walking while Tabitha stared at her blood-soaked hands. Her dull gaze soon shifted to angst as she looked at Anton. "What kind of monster murders a child?"

Near rabid and practically foaming at the mouth, Tabitha stood up and pointed at him as if her finger were an extension of a maniacal blade. At that moment, a surge wafted through her – a flow that altered her dark tresses – a distortion that changed the color of her blonde hair to red before it settled into a hypnotic blue flame hue, rippling in the wind like a sail out at sea. The powerful pulsations transcended in such a way that they tore Anton's clothes off piece-by-piece and when there was no fabric left to remove, the enigmatic pulse tore into his flesh; blood flailed from his ravaged body like wet paint tossed about in gale-force winds.

The assault progressed to his muscles and eventually his tendons, disbanding them one by one until all that was left of him was his still beating heart suspended in mid-air and by the end of her tirade, all that was left of him was polished bone.

The ground began to tremble ferociously and the trees began to whine under the pressure.

Moments later, his heart imploded. During the horrific process, the color of her eyes intensified before it flickered into a typical brown shade. The shudders turned vicious, and with it, storm clouds congregated overhead. Draíocht Dol became a tumultuous place. The ruthless decadence of thunder rolling coupled with the crack of lightning painted the sky like nothing they'd ever seen before. Moments later, they heard a rumbling sound that got louder by the second until the disruptive element advanced at full force towards them, leaving no time for them to react. With her mouth agape, Tabitha was about to say, '*Run!*' just as the 30-foot wave crashed into the area, swiping them off their feet, an impact felt well beyond their shores.

After nature had its tantrum, public officials and reporters alike traveled to Draíocht Dol to survey the damage and returned to relay the news. It wasn't until days later when Mr. Kingsley sat in his study sipping tea that he read the headline of the newspaper Lenard brought in earlier, *Freak Wave Kills Everyone on Draíocht Dol.*

"Lenard … have they returned?"

"No, sir."

He glanced at his watch. "That'll be all."

He made a mental note to send letters of condolence to their families and then proceeded to write a draft for tomorrow's classifieds, *Help wanted – good pay but the applicant must be willing to do anything. What a tragedy*, Mr. Kingsley thought and shook his head.

10

The wave receded from Draíocht Dol reducing the island to a marshland with a few dilapidated structures and seemingly no inhabitants. The debris that remained washed up on the shores of Vermouthshire and Aerona and wildlife flocked there. The destruction was unprecedented and it warranted a massive cleanup.

Whereas, south of the island, seabirds swooned above the swollen carcass of a horse lying on the coastline; a mere apparition of its former self. Further down the beach, a man laid face down in the sand. The tide came up, wetted him up to his chest and receded. Another wave came ashore, a stronger one that sent water well above his head and forced liquid into his nose and mouth inducing a gag reflex. He spat profusely and came up on his knees just as the forceful wave knocked him sideways. Lacking the strength to stand, he crawled on his belly to a shaded area beneath a tree, flipped over on his back, and lost consciousness.

Hours later, he opened his eyes but strangely, he couldn't see the sky. At first, everything was blurry but once his vision improved - a figure became clear. He was still lying down but in bed and to his left, a woman stood at his bedside in a pristine white dress and matching white cap looking at him. Her soulful blue eyes drew him in, and the radiance she exuded gave life to an otherwise dull room that reeked of cleaning supplies.

He tried to move but everything ached and an undeniable throbbing pain persisted. He managed to lift his head, although when he tried to move his arm, he inadvertently yanked the intravenous line attached to his right forearm.

"Hi. I'm Samantha. You're at St. Vincent's Hospital. I'll be the nurse caring for you today." She adjusted the sheet around his body.

"How did I get here?" his voice cracked as he spoke.

"A worker from the disaster clean-up crew found you unconscious on a beach."

"Was I alone?"

"I don't know … but if you don't mind me asking, how did you come to be there?" she asked from the edge of the bed.

"I got swept away when the wave hit Draíocht Dol."

Her forehead creased. "You might not remember me, but I was the nurse who tended to you the last time." She paused and then snickered briefly. "You must've left a bad taste in the sea's mouth. If I'm not mistaken, this is the second time that it's spat you out." Samantha turned to walk away but then she stopped and turned to him.

"Did you ever get your memory back?"

"No … I didn't. They said there is a chance that it may never return."

"Well, I hope it does. I can't imagine going through life not knowing who I am or where I came from. So what name do you go by?"

"Bryson."

"Regardless of the circumstances, it's nice to see you again."

A curl slipped from her cap and fell to her cheek. Her stunned expression gave way to an awkward smile that temporarily locked her in his gaze.

"Likewise." He tried to sit up in the bed and slumped back to the mattress.

She lessened the distance between them. "Would you like me to adjust the bed? Or perhaps get you another pillow?"

"Both please."

"I'll be right back." Samantha left the room and returned with a pillow, adjusted the bed and propped it behind his head.

"Is that better?" she asked with care.

"It's perfect. Thank you."

"If all goes well, you'll be discharged tomorrow but only if you pass the physical exam."

"I'll be sure to study," he said and laughed. She chuckled briefly.

"Get some rest. You'll do fine. Well …" Samantha fiddled with her fingers like a woman waiting for a kiss. "It's nearing the end of my shift but another nurse will be along shortly to assist you."

"Will you be here tomorrow?"

"I'm off, but you'll be in good hands," and with that said she exited the room.

•••

The following day, a nurse took his vital signs and left the room. Shortly afterward, the doctor entered and did his examination.

"Everything looks good. Just take it easy for about a week or two and I think you'll be fine. I'll get your discharge papers ready." He jotted down some notes in Bryson's chart, left the room, and returned a short time later with his release papers.

Having been discharged, Bryson stood outside of St. Vincent's Hospital eager to get a taxi out of there. He saw one parked across the street and hailed it. The cab came around to him and rolled down the window. "Where-you-going?" he asked in one breath.

"Clod Hill." Bryson got in and the cab pulled away from the hospital.

Once they neared Clod hill, he breathed a sigh of relief. It was then that the incident that took place at the O'Brien's residence came back to him. He knew Anton could be a brute at times but he hadn't expected him to take a life. Especially when he considered the fact that Anton was the person who found him on the sandy shores of Vermouthshire three years ago. He had transported him to the hospital and once he'd recovered, offered him a place to stay and referred him for the job opening at the Kingsley's mansion. Even though he'd done a good deed, Anton crossed the line and committed a heinous act – damage that couldn't be undone. Bryson blinked away tears and sighed. Moments later, the cab parked outside the mansion, he paid, walked up to the front door and rang the doorbell.

The butler's eyes widened as he opened the door. "Well, I'll be damned! We thought you were dead."

"Good afternoon to you too," Bryson said and entered.

"My apologies, sir … we heard that there were no survivors."

"I get it. Is Mr. Kingsley in?"

"Yes. He's in the study." Lenard went ahead of him and announced his arrival. Shortly thereafter, he exited the study. "Mr. Kingsley will see you."

Bryson entered the room.

"Well—look who's come back from the dead. Only a chosen few can say that."

"Boasting about those things are pointless, sir. Many lives were lost, including Anton and Gill's."

"I know. I mailed out letters of condolences to their families along with their severance pay."

"That was kind of you, sir."

"It was the least I could do."

"Did you guys meet with Mr. O'Brien?"

"We did. He didn't change his mind so Anton killed his son. Then the next thing I knew, all hell broke loose."

Kingsley sat there palming his chin. "That's unfortunate, but it's the price he paid for defying me."

Bryson's jaw stiffened.

"What became of the rest of the family?" he said, anxiously rubbing his hands together.

"The wave washed us away shortly after Anton shot the boy. As far as I know, I'm the only survivor."

"Great! The last thing I need is a litigation suit and police officers snooping around my affairs. Take the week off, but after that, report to work. You are free to go."

"Thank you, sir." Bryson left the study.

By not chastising Anton or Gill's actions Mr. Kingsley condoned them. Bryson shook his head on the way out and walked down the hall to the exit. He went out the front door where he saw the chauffeur standing at the car door; Bryson went over, got in. Once the car drove down the hill, he exhaled as if he were holding his breath since he arrived.

He went home to a windowless room that he rented in a twenty-six-room apartment building, laid on a twin size bed in a room barely large enough to hold a bed and a suitcase, and stared at the ceiling until he fell asleep. Moments later, in an all too real dream, he recalled the day that he and Anton traveled to Draíocht Dol. Actually, there was a time when Anton returned from a solo trip reeking of gasoline and smoke. Bryson didn't think much of it at the time, but he did notice that the O'Brien's shop was burned down. After realizing how devious his employer, was Bryson began to wonder if there was more to what took place. At the same time, other long lost familial things surfaced of people and places that he'd long forgotten.

A reel of unfamiliar silhouettes projected from the black of his eyes of people waiting to board a ship. The womans face that was foreign to him, and yet seeing her calmed him. Her luminous dark-brown hair flowed like angelic threads moving in symphony with the wind and the few strands of hair that grazed him felt like the finest silk. The images soon faded but the woman lingered, holding him as he stood at a seaside port and slowly a man materialized holding a boy's hand. They shed many tears as they embraced one another and then parted ways. This visualization also faded, but not before, he heard the woman say. "We love you, Uri," she yelled as he navigated the narrow gangway to the ship. At that moment, he woke gasping.

11

What he'd seen in his dreams kept him up for much of the night, countless hours in which snippets of his memories came in successions like raindrops on his forehead preceded by a slow dissemination of information through the keyhole of his mind. His memories returned like a long lost friend, an event that triggered convulsions. He remembered boarding the Genesis en route to Astonia. However, during the journey the ship encountered a Nor'easter that ravaged the vessel, causing considerable damage. The passengers on the first and second level boarded the lifeboats, leaving the passengers in steerage onboard to fend for themselves. Those left behind clung together, bound by fear, waiting for their untimely end.

Despite the Genesis' grandness, it was no match for Mother Nature: the vessel tipped, and those who were still aboard went down with the ship. All the people in the lifeboats could do was watch the devastation unfold and wait for rescue ships to come. After days of wading in the surf with no ships in sight, death seemed kinder but only when it was off somewhere visiting someone else, not up close and personal staring them in the face. After a time, even the lifeboats sunk to the depths of the sea. Some passengers tried to float like lilies, but the ferocious waves doused them, filling their orifices with brine and ultimately lowering them like steel anchors to the depths of the sea – their lifeless eyes staring at the deep while they sunk. Despite the tendency of an ill-fated outcome, he weathered the storm, swam with and not against the waves until he gave into exhaustion. By then, the waves saw it fit to toss him onto Vermouthshire's shore.

。。。

Unlike Vermouthshire and Draíocht Dol, Aerona's coarse sand and harsh terrain picked the bones of many who did not live to tell the tales of their misfortune. For decades, many ships had wrecked on the reef-like island. When it faded behind the fog, it seemingly disappeared from sight, which gave oncoming ships the 'all clear' only to end up amongst a graveyard of ships. On that very day, a dense fog skulked over Aerona, but the sole cabin on the island always remained visible for miles like a lighthouse atop Caroline Hill.

A draft disturbed the shreds of the fabric of her layered mesh dress. Solara was the custodian of Aerona, a temperamental island unwilling to allow any human other than her to colonize it—it was content with her and the creatures that found refuge there. She strolled on the shoreline scanning for anything of value. As of late, a few valuables had washed up on its shores – backwash from the freak wave. Solara stood still when she noticed something lying ahead. She approached, knelt, and put her index finger to the side of the neck. In all the years she'd inhabited the island today was different, this one had a pulse.

"The island must like you," she gripped. "I'm not built for this." She was far from agile, and yet

Solara gathered the strength to lift the limp body and carried her discovery home.

Weary from the task, she sat in her favorite chair by the bed and peered at her visitor who was sleeping deeper than anyone she'd ever seen. Nevertheless, Solara looked after her uninvited guest waiting for any change. Strangely, ever since she brought her guest home, the sensation of someone tapping on her shoulder began and persisted.

Days later, she sighed. "It's about that time," she moaned as she got up from the rocking chair, and grabbed her cane on the way out.

The timeworn recluse walked the coastline savoring the smell of the salt in the wind and the wistful sea breeze tussling through her silken hair. Her only disappointment was that she found nothing of value. She scaled the stone embankment to her cabin and opened the door to see an empty bed.

Solara sat in her chair. "You'll be back," she said and rocked until she got sleepy.

As Solara nodded off to sleep, outdoors her guest wildly scanned the landscape outdoors with a crown of brush and garments painted with muck. A cloaked man emerged from the mist with skin that likened to the bark of a tree in every direction her guest turned the man seemingly encircling, and around him, a symphony of unnerving snarls, sobs, and shrieks enveloped the area. Her guest sprinted through a collection of trees, which faded as she sought shelter there. Running nowhere fast proved maddening but the only thing that brought solace was her feet landing on solid ground.

Ahead, the sporadic illumination of a cabin on the slope warping each time it flickered caused Solara's guest to stand still. After releasing a sigh, she returned to the cabin and touched the logs to be sure that it was there. Perhaps it was a dream because nothing made sense there. Disappearing trees, men made of bark, and yet the cabin was tangible? She shut her eyes and opened them again, and then opened the door. The moment she stepped inside, the ground gave way from beneath her, and a never-ending space-time continual drop began her eyes clenched as what felt like every organ in her body shuffling for what seem like an eternity until she crumpled to the floor. Too afraid to move she hesitantly opened her eyes. On her hands and knees, she looked up at Solara sitting in the rocking chair.

"Welcome back."

She gulped as she caught sight of a gargantuan bullfrog ogling her as it croaked while seated on a shelf beside a collection of large jars filled with worms, beetles, and all breeds of snakes. The shelf resting against a sedimentary rock wall covered in moss that likened to tapestry and between it, laid wood columns. It's craterous, pasty green skin fluctuated to various shades of green.

"Where am I?" she tried not to make eye contact with Solara.

"You're on Aerona. Did she scare you?" she asked in a condescending tone. Knowing fully well that the island had played mind games with her – purely for its own amusement but otherwise, its peculiarities served as a protective barrier that ensured the safety of Aerona's inhabitants.

Her eyes expanded in their sockets. "She did. What is this place?"

Solara chuckled, "It's a haven where mystics can live in peace."

"How did I get here?" she asked.

"I found you lying on the beach. Where did you come from?"

"Draíocht Dol."

"I see … that explains it; the wave must have brought you here."

At the same time, memories of the last day on Draíocht Dol brought her to tears, which developed into the cries of someone who had experienced an ultimate loss. "My son," she cried out, "they killed my son."

The sensation on Solara's shoulder increased. "Who are you?"

"Tabitha O'Brien."

Solara stood and Tabitha gazed at the tall, eerie woman, but actually Solara was no more than five feet but to others, she was an imposing 6 feet 4 inches tall.

"What are you? I've been getting an odd feeling ever since I found you."

"I'm Tabitha—"

"What are you?" Solara interrupted.

Tabitha sat there silent staring into her cloudy eyes for a while. "I don't know."

"Do you ... how should I put this ... can you do things that no one else is capable of doing?"

Her teeth tapped as she searched for words.

"You can tell me anything. Nothing is new under the sun," Solara assured.

Tabitha lowered her head. "Strange things happen when I engage with objects that are linked to other realms. For example, over the past year, I allowed a spirit to help us recover from a difficult transition. Things began to look up. Our crops

115

flourished, we had more than we could eat, an abundance that led to a business venture."

Solara nodded. "But at what price?"

"It's funny you'd ask, he just wanted to help but his wife had other motives. They wanted children but never got the chance to start their family, so she desired to be a mother figure to my son." A lone tear trailed down Tabitha's cheek.

"Was he the son that you lost?" Solara asked rocking in her chair.

"Yes. He was killed moments before the wave hit."

Solara exhaled and sat deeper in the chair. "Did you live up to your end of the bargain?"

"For the most part, yes …" Then she recalled her last encounter with him. "Actually … I didn't and he expressed his frustrations the day before Jon's death. Marc didn't know about any of this."

"Did you summon him, or did he come to you?"

"He came while I tried to contact another spirit."

"Ahh, I see," Solara said. Tabitha stiffened.

"Did you use your abilities to avenge your son's death?"

"Actually … I did, just before the wave hit."

"Your eyes, they're brown but as I look deeper, I see red." At that very moment, Solara's skin fluctuated in color before it settled into its natural shade and Tabitha felt as though the air was sucked out of the room. "How did you—"

"They said you would come - but some of us thought that you were a myth." She miffed poignantly. "Tabitha O'Brien, you are a superlative being, a sorceress of unmistakable power."

"Sorceress?" Tabitha laughed it off.

"Denying it won't change what you are. Besides, you have a bigger problem on your hands. An imp, a mischievous being with dark intent has attached itself to you. I believe that Albert played a role in everything that's unfolded since you last saw him. How much, I'm not sure, but I'll say this; if you had kept up with your end of the bargain, no harm would have come to your son." Solara got up from her chair and began to pace the room.

"It all makes sense now. When a sorcerer uses their power without the benefit of knowing its strength, their power can be an unruly conductor and have devastating effects. Be careful; there isn't anything that you cannot influence, though I should say that one should never meddle with the sands of time."

Solara's staff came down with force as it connected with the floor, causing the ground beneath them to quake. Just then, the door flew open, and the windows fissured, forming hairline fractures. After that, the dishes on the counter skipped off the edge one by one and crashed to the floor. And the large glass jars that she saw earlier on the shelf shattered, sending an assortment of creepy crawling things slithering throughout the room. Tabitha pranced about to avoid stepping on them but she found herself backed into a corner surrounded by them. She clenched her eyes and started to mumble. When she opened them again, there was nothing there.

Moments later, Solara's ghastly image transformed into a docile woman with long golden hair, dressed in a long embroidered tunic-style dress and sandals. The once dreary walls in the cabin gave way to soft colors and vases of fresh flowers stationed throughout the room on accent tables, quieting her fears.

"You and I are alike. I am a sorcerer too. It was foretold that a magical being would come with eyes as red as blood. I've waited many lifetimes for this moment to come. So, fear not, your safe within these walls."

12

Bryson's gut babbled as he lay in bed recovering day after day while the delectable aroma of food seeped through the walls from other rooms, and yet it did little to heighten his desire to eat. He just lied there staring at the wall without blinking. Before he knew it, a week had gone by and it was time to return to work, and yet he couldn't bring himself to go. The knowledge that he'd unsuspectingly played a part in the demise of his family crippled him. Although he found a sliver of solace when he remembered what their life was like when they inhabited on *Ládonia,* but no matter how hard he tried, images of their demise skulked in and took hold of his subconscious, paralyzing him with the truth.

Bryson mustered what little strength he had to sit up, got a sheet of paper, wrote a short paragraph and closed with his signature. He put it in an envelope, got dressed and caught a cab to the Kingsley Mansion. An hour later, the car pulled into the mansion's driveway; Bryson ambled to the front door and knocked.

Lenard greeted him. "Good afternoon, sir. It's nice to see you out and about."

"Thank you, Lenard. Is Mr. Kingsley in?"

"He should be finishing up with Mr. Newman any minute now."

Bryson's brow arched.

"He's the new bodyguard."

As he traveled down the hall, his attention diverted to a man of average height and musculature a shorter brawnier version of Anton, but of equally icy disposition with an olive skin tone and a baby face coming his way. Their eyes briefly met before Mr. Newman turned banked the corner at the end of the corridor near the front door.

"I'll let Mr. Kingsley know that you're here." Lenard walked down the hall and entered the study. A short time later, he returned with a tray of empty liquor glasses and approached Bryson.

"Mr. Kingsley will see you."

121

Bryson traveled down the hall and entered the study, "Good afternoon, sir."

"Good afternoon. I hope all is well with your health?"

"I'm better." Bryson cleared his throat and retrieved the letter he wrote from the breast pocket of his jacket. "I came to give you this." Kingsley took the letter and read it as he sat at his desk.

He looked over the top of the letter at Bryson and then he flung the paper aside. "You wish to end your employment?"

"Yes, sir. I think it's time to move on."

"And what do you plan to do afterward?"

"I haven't decided yet, but I know that I don't want to do this anymore," Bryson said firmly.

"Very well … is there anything else you'd like to say?"

"Actually, there is. Has there been any news about Gill or Anton?"

"Yes … they found them the day after you were here last. Gill's body was found in decent

122

shape considering the manner of which he perished, but Anton wasn't so lucky. The condition of his body was like that of someone who had been exposed to the elements for decades instead of days."

Strangely, Bryson found his response gratifying. However, he wasn't surprised about Anton's condition – after all he'd seen it firsthand. As far as he was concerned, Anton got exactly what he deserved.

13

Bryson left Kingsley's office and walked down the hall feeling like a burden had been lifted, and more so when he stepped outside the front door; he felt something he hadn't felt in a while—free. He exhaled and walked to the gated entrance and passed the chauffeur as he wiped off the car. He looked up when Bryson was about to walk through the gate.

"Bryson," he yelled. Bryson looked back at him.

He gestured for him to come. Bryson went over to the garage. "Where are you going?"

"Downtown."

"I can take you if you hold on until I finish the car."

"You don't have to."

"I insist. It's no trouble at all. Are you done for the day?"

"I'm done period. I resigned."

The chauffeur nodded. "I see." He wiped the last bit of water from the car.

Shortly afterward, they drove down Clod Hill at a high rate of speed causing his stomach to flop. He gazed out the window watching the scenery slip by and promised himself that he'd never return to this place. They approached the border where the town and countryside met, resulting in a drastic change in scenery – a lively ambiance with the sails standing out in the distance above the rooftops in the backdrop.

"Make a left on Lick Liver Drive."

No further instructions were necessary, the driver knew exactly where to go. He made the turn and parked moments outside of The Social Nomad.

"Thank you." Bryson stepped out of the car.

"Take care," the chauffeur said and drove away.

Daisy crossed paths with him as he entered, "Welcome to The Social Nomad."

An awkward smile surfaced as he got a glimpse of the beautiful mountains she had – breasts, which made him think back on Mr. Finkelsteen's story from weeks earlier. He chuckled lightly and shifted his gaze elsewhere. He went over to the bar. Ben stood behind the counter refilling a glass at the far end and then made the journey over to Bryson.

"What are you having?"

"A beer." Bryson looked at his reflection in the mirror as Ben poured the beer and put it on a coaster in front of him.

"Heard about your friend. He was a ruffian but a likable," Ben said.

Bryson nodded and took a drink, which sent the gas bubbles in his stomach into a rampage. A burning sensation inched up his throat. The beer was the last thing he should consume on an empty stomach. He signaled for the bartender.

"How much do I owe you?"

"Two dollars."

Bryson paid, left the bar and strolled down Lick Liver Drive but came to an abrupt stop, bent over and puked pure liquid. He stood there holding onto the lamppost and soon after felt as though someone was watching him. Bryson regained his composure and looked in that direction. Seeing her invigorated him.

"It's nice to see you in something other than a hospital gown," Samantha said.

He laughed under his breath. "I think I look pretty good in those gowns."

"Do you live around here?" They began a walk side by side down the sidewalk.

"Yes, in an apartment complex not far from the harbor."

"Really? I live around there too." He smiled.

"Would you like to have lunch with me?"

Samantha stopped walking and looked at him, "Are you asking me out?"

"I hope I'm not stepping on anyone's toes," he backtracked fearing that he'd read her wrong.

"I'm single," she said without hesitation.

He opened the door and entered the small eatery after her. They sat at a table by the window and chatted. During their conversation, he shared with her that he had quit his job. Immediately thereafter, he regretted it. After all, he gathered that women didn't find an unemployed man appealing but he felt comfortable enough that he could tell her anything but he drew the line at telling her about the horrific murder that he witnessed.

"It's getting dark. Do you mind if I walk you home?" Bryson asked, peering into her blue eyes.

"I'd like that." Samantha wiped the corners of her mouth with the napkin and placed it on the table.

He gestured for the server. "I'd like the bill please."

A short time later, the server returned with the bill. He paid and they left the eatery. By then, the temperature had dropped considerably with a lingering chill in the air.

"I had a lovely time." She looked at him from the side and smiled.

The urge to jump and click his heels was hard to shake when he heard that. "I'm glad you enjoyed our time together. Maybe we can do this again another time?"

She beamed. "I'd like that."

He bent his elbow, she hooked her hand in his, and they walked while enjoying each other up until they arrived at the entrance of her building.

"Well, I'm going in. I look forward to seeing you soon."

He let go of her hand and kept his eyes on her even though they'd parted. "I do too. Well, I ought to head home."

Bryson entered the building next door, went up to his room, undressed and laid in bed. It was then that Anton's words came back to him, 'Mr. Kingsley doesn't like to hear no.' His body tensed. Quitting his job wasn't the same thing and yet he couldn't shake the feeling that perhaps it qualified.

Later that afternoon, a loud commotion echoed in the hallway. Bryson cracked his door and peeked out, his eyes widening when he spotted Mr. Newman five doors down kicking in a door. He quietly closed the door, dressed in a hurry and eased his way out of the room.

The racket of objects being tossed about and landing permeated the hall as he inched toward the room where Newman was wreaking havoc on his way to the exit. There was no way around it; it was the only way to get to the exit. He made it past the room, but not without Newman getting a glimpse of him.

"Hey you!" Newman shouted as Bryson bolted out the entrance and narrowly missed colliding with a couple entering. With no time to extend apologies, Bryson kept going - his life depended on it.

He ran toward the harbor were dusk darkened the vista beyond the shore and when reached hallway, he looked back. Newman was a half block behind but closing in fast. Bryson took off again but eventually ran out of places to run to once he approached the pier. He could either swim or chance it and catch a boat that was already pushing away from the docks. Neither option was appealed to him; he fidgeted while he contemplated what to do but then he heard Newman's footfalls landing as he ran on the boardwalk. He exhaled heavily and ran full speed ahead to a small boat near the end of the dock, lifting the tarp covering the boat and flattening himself as he climbed in.

"Damn it," Newman shouted as he made it midway of the wharf.

Close enough that Bryson heard him griping. It wasn't how he planned on spending his evening, but the hull of the small vessel was better than the finality of a casket. He couldn't risk leaving, the location might be under surveillance, and he couldn't go back to his apartment so the boat, albeit uncomfortable was his best bet to get through the night.

For much of the night, he dwelled on notions of life and death until the rhythmic waves of the ocean rocked him to sleep.

A thought provoking night progressed into a noisy morning as the ship's crew chatted and walked about as they readied to leave the port. The dock area grew silent; moments later, he was doused with cold water. As the chilly water hit him his eyes flew open; a scruffy old man stood above him with a bucket.

"What are you doing in my boat?"

Bryson spat off to the side of the boat and didn't bother to reply.

"Get off of my boat."

"Shh." Bryson put his index finger to his lips. "Lower your voice, please. Someone is trying to kill me."

The bearded man looking down at him sighed. "Look, I don't care. Get out of my boat and we'll forget that this ever happened."

"Please. I need to get off this island. I don't have much on me but I will give you all that I have."

He scratched his scruffy beard. "All right, but you're paddling."

"That's fine with me," Bryson replied without hesitation. The scruffy old man untied the boat and they set sail. "Where are you going?"

"Fishing off the coast of Aerona."

Bryson rowed until his arms were sore and by then the waves grew rough. "It's getting pretty bad. Maybe we should head back," he advised pausing briefly to stretch his arms.

"Didn't you say someone was trying to kill you?" He gave Bryson a smug look.

"Yes, but I don't want to escape one grave to occupy another."

"All right, young man. I'll take over from here." He took the oars and paddled north of the coast of Aerona. The waves were even higher on that end and within no time at all, water filled the hull. His soiled britches further reminded him that he and the sea that did agree. Meanwhile, a fog skulked above the surface of the ocean obstructing their view, but the old man continued onward. A lengthy drawn out scratching sound, then a dull, gaudy thump resonated moments before the boat crumbled into the sea.

14

He could feel his entire body ache when he moved and opened his eyes soon after. His hands were awkwardly tied behind his back and knees weighing down the sand beneath him. He tried to wiggle his way free, but his hands were bound tightly. Hogtied and disoriented he peeked out of the corner of his eye at a tall, hideous woman with long gray hair standing in front of him holding a staff in her hand.

"Let me go," he pleaded.

"Two intruders in less than two weeks ... this is getting interesting," Solara said to herself.

She dragged him across the sand, chafing his tummy raw along the way. In exchange, he got front row seats to view countless pin sized teeth gnawing at the edge of her lengthy ashen hair. Dragged senseless, he felt his binding loosening broke free and quickly ran for his life. Seconds into his sprint, he ran out of sand and found himself suspended just above the thorn-infested ground. With her use of simple gestures of the hand, Solara pulled him back into submission and beckoned the ropes simultaneously to bind his legs and hands. From there on out, he didn't fight his restraints and quietly observed as she pulled him up the slope to the cabin. She dropped him like a sack of potatoes just inside the cabin's door. In agonizing pain and yet he had no energy to cry out as he hit the floor. He lay there peering at the wall ahead, and strangely, with every blink, the walls warped, even though nothing had changed. Throughout the dreary expanse, the dull drone of water flowing from a faucet rebounded, and yet there was none in the room. Then, slime dropped from the ceiling closely followed by wretched screams that engulfed the room and dulled his senses.

Then, the hiss of an effortless slider came from the corner of the room as the large cobra flared the flap of the skin that adorned its head. Instinctively, Bryson made himself small as the Cobra darted forward.

"Easy boy," Solara said. She threw a snack and the snake wrapped its tongue around it and sucked it in like spaghetti.

"Good boy. Now sit," she commanded; the cobra laid flat with its eyes set on Bryson.

He looked on in disbelief while icy water falling from the ceiling landed on his shoulder. He looked up; large stalactites hung like bats, dripping ancient tears. To his right, a woman much younger than the old hag with silky brown hair sat with her back to him. At the same time, a lightheaded feeling came over him and before he knew it, he lost consciousness.

Solara sat at the table with her. "We have a visitor. You're no longer the only one to survive this ravenous island."

Tabitha put a spoon full of porridge in her mouth. "Um-hmm," she mumbled and an urge to look over her shoulder surfaced, so she did. A bound young man lied on the floor. "You should be nicer to your guests."

"If I did, they'd stay longer and I don't want that."

Tabitha chuckled, "He appears to be ill. Release him."

"And if I do and he tries to attack us what then?"

"You can turn him into a salamander if you choose to, but free him," Tabitha pleaded. She dropped her spoon and left the cabin.

Solara sighed, "Wonder what's eating her?" She untied him and rested him on the bed. "Gosh! You stink. You have some nerve bringing that god-awful odor into my home."

She undressed him, and while doing so trailed her index finger down the center of his chest, savoring every millimeter of his young flesh, but her hand stopped short of his britch-line. She couldn't remember when last she'd seen or touched a chest this taut ... perhaps epochs ago? "Ah, to be young and carefree," Solara shook her head and smiled as she sponged him off, but left

138

him untouched from the waist down and left him to air dry.

Long after she'd cleaned him, a fever took hold that caused his tongue to run amok, rambling on about boats, men with guns, and death. Solara sat there listening to him and decoded his message all while a warm feeling came over her. Alas, the mischievous island had shown a side she'd never seen; compassion brought her to tears which caused the horrific guise in the room to diminish allowing the beautiful haven to shine through.

Tabitha entered the cabin. "Your guard is down." She noticed the tears running down Solara's cheeks. "What's wrong?"

"Nothing, for a change." She dabbed her eyes with a handkerchief.

"Go over and see how he's doing." She didn't bother to question Solara.

Tabitha went over and sat at the edge of the bed. Shortly afterward, his eyes fluttered and then opened completely. He looked at her with a blank expression on his face. *Death has finally come.* He exhaled; *this is it - my punishment, this is her spirit acting as the gatekeeper to the afterlife. If so, I take my judgment. I'll freely walk into the flames for my part in his undoing.*

"Uri?" she asked with a perturbed look on her face that was quickly replaced with infinite joy.

"Mother, is that really you?"

She pulled away, but he held onto her torso and bawled like a child. The last time she called his name was when she tried to summon him and instead Albert reared his head. She understood now why he hadn't come—he was alive. Her hand trembled as she touched his face. Tears fell one after the other as they sobbed while they held onto each other for dear life.

"They said you were dead … that the sea swallowed you whole," she managed to say before giving way to sobs.

Thereafter, the twitch of recollection came over her and instantaneously her gaze turned fierce. "Wait a minute. Weren't you one of the men who came to the cabin?" She edged away from him as her rage intensified.

"It's not what you think. I did not know what they had planned. I tried to stop him. You remember, don't you?"

"I remember you standing by while a man shot your brother in the gut!"

"Mother, please I wouldn't harm anyone. I survived the Genesis, but my memory didn't; I had no idea that Mr. Kingsley gave Anton the go-ahead to kill anyone who stood in his way." He hung his head in shame.

"The wave that hit Draíocht Dol swept me away and I washed up on the shore in Vermouthshire. As I said before, my memory returned but only after being recently discharged from the hospital. I was shamefaced, mortified when I realized that I played a part in the demise of my brother. I hope you can bring yourself to forgive me."

She fell to her knees and stared impatiently at the floor.

"Tabitha, forgive. The island has given you an ultimate gift. Don't take it for granted," Solara said as calm as possible and gazed at Uri. "I see no malice in his eyes. He's telling the truth."

Uri came off the bed; he knelt at Tabitha's feet and put his arms around her. "I'm sorry for everything that you've gone through. If I could take it back I would." She rested her head on his shoulder.

Her lips quivered as she spoke, "I forgive you, son."

Solara observed as they made amends, a moment that brought tears to her eyes. Relieved that he'd been forgiven and seeing Tabitha being reunited with her son, it seemed like the unyielding sob fest would never end but eventually, it tapered off. After a while, he let go of her and they spent the rest of the night gazing at each other.

"Your eyes ..." his forehead rippled. "They've changed."

Tabitha sighed, "It changed after I'd used my powers to avenge Jon's death. They're brown now, I'm content with that and I hope it stays that way. I don't have to hide anymore. I can walk around without people staring at me."

"Your eyes didn't bother me. In some way, they calmed me. I remember looking into them for hours when I was a child until I'd fall asleep," Uri said in a daydream gaze.

"Things were going so well for us but it wasn't enough for me. I longed for you."

"How have you been?" she asked and held his hand.

"Lonely. Not knowing my identity didn't make it any easier so I work a lot. And when I wasn't, I'd stare at strangers, hoping that someone would recognize me or that a memory would return to release me from the incredible emptiness that I felt." He wanted to say more, tell her about Anton and how he had helped him, but that would only add insult to her injury.

15

Tabitha gazed at him filled with new purpose. "Take me to Mr. Kingsley," she said sternly.

The last thing he wanted to hear, let alone do. "It's too dangerous." He stood up and paced the room. "I don't want to lose you."

"I'm quite capable of defending myself," she reminded him.

"I know, but bullets are swift. They have no respect for the lives that they take. Please, abandon your plans."

"I can't."

Powerless against her demands, he gave in to her and mentally prepared himself for what was to come.

"Solara, do you have a boat that we can borrow?"

Solara fanned herself with a large dried sea grape leaf glued to a stick. She huffed, "Does a beach have sand?"

144

"Do you have a boat or not?" she asked impatiently.

"It's below the cliff at the side of the cabin."

"You aren't going to make this easy are you?"

"Why should I? I've been waiting for you for decades, and now that you're here, you want to go off and right wrongs that can't be undone."

"I'll be the judge of that," Tabitha said and marched out the door with Uri trailing her.

"Wait a minute! Aren't you going to change your clothing?"

Tabitha stopped and turned to her. "Have you forgotten that I washed up on this island with nothing but the clothes on my back?" Tabitha and Uri returned to the cabin and closed the door.

"I haven't." Solara went over to her closet and made a selection. "Here." She took the lavender dress Solara gave her.

"You can't walk into a mansion wearing rags. They'll think you're a beggar. Take these too." Solara gave her a pair of spool boots and stockings to complete her look.

145

She went into the other room and changed into the dress; its low square neckline, cuffed sleeves, and tapered bodice, with a full frilled skirt, accentuated her figure. Afterward, she looked in the mirror thinking, *I could easily pass for an upper-class citizen.*

"Will the island allow us to leave?"

"If I didn't think it would, we wouldn't be having this conversation."

Shortly after their conversation, they left the cabin, walked around the back and looked below the cliff. It was a long way down, but thankfully, there were railed stairs that led to a small dock. They walked down the steep steps, clinging to the railing as the wind cast tendrils of her hair into his face. The poor lad had to clear his face repeatedly in order to see where his footfalls should land.

"Are we really going to do this?"

Tabitha was through with the questions; she stayed mute and descended the steps.

They made it safely to the bottom, boarded the boat and the wind carried them away from Aerona toward Vermouthshire.

"There's something you should know before we step foot on Vermouthshire."

"What is it son?"

"Mr. Kingsley's goon tried to kill me. That's why I left Vermouthshire and the reason why I ended up in Aerona."

"I'm sorry to hear that, but there's no need to worry. No harm will come to you, I promise."

Even with her assurance, he didn't feel safe. After all, Jon died in her arms. She couldn't save him, how could she protect him? So, he prepared himself for what was to come. He lowered the sail as they neared the wharf, coasted in, and tied the boat to the dock.

She took in the scenery at the busy harbor where fancy ships waited for their captains and passengers anxiously waited to be taken out to sea. They sauntered down the wharf's boardwalk to the downtown area passing stylish shops.

Tabitha peered out beyond the hilly landscape in the distance and then her attention returned to the well-dressed people walking about.

She spotted him from a half a block away and called out to him, "Bryson." Oblivious to her summons, he continued walking down the sidewalk.

"Bryson," this time she shouted louder. He stopped and looked behind him. Tabitha, a few steps ahead of him stopped as well.

She ran to him, "I'm so glad you're okay. I overheard the maintenance man next door talking to someone outside my building about damage sustained in your room and across the hall. No one had seen you since that day. I was so worried," she said out of breath.

"I'm fine."

"Uri, let's go," Tabitha stated impatiently.

Samantha beheld the beautiful, elegantly dressed, dark-haired woman, "Forgive me. I'm sorry. I didn't realize that you were with someone." Her expression soured; Samantha turned to walk away from him.

"It's not what you think," he grabbed her hand. She looked over her shoulder at him.

"She's my mother," he clarified. Samantha tried to conceal her joy when he said that.

"I have to go, but we'll talk later." He turned away from her and walked toward Tabitha who'd already begun to walk away.

Uri followed, dragging his feet as he hailed a taxi.

"Where to?" he asked.

"Clod Hill." They drove on the hilly terrain leading up to Clod Hill.

A woozy feeling surfaced in the pit of his stomach. "Stop the car. I can't do this." The color of his face bordering on blue.

"Stop it! You're making yourself ill."

"Mother ... please, let's go home," he pleaded.

"Home?" Her voice elevated an octave. There's no *home* to go to, thanks to Mr. Kingsley everything your father, brother, and I worked for is gone."

A short time later, the mansion came into view. Moments later, they were on Clod Hill entering the circular driveway at the front of the structure.

She was calm for someone walking into a lion's den. On the other hand, Uri was shaking, all he could fathom was the mouth of a guillotine. He felt as though his only chance for escape was the taxi. They exited the car, walked to the front door, and rang the bell.

Lenard answered the door. "Bryson, I thought we'd seen the last of you."

"That was the plan," he replied forcing a smile.

"Are you here to see Mr. Kingsley?"

"Not today. I'm escorting ..."

"Mrs. Ryan." Tabitha filled in. "I'd like to meet with Mr. Kingsley concerning a business proposition."

"Is he expecting you Ma'am?" Lenard inquired.

"No, but I do believe that he'd hate to miss out on a promising offer."

Uri stood silently on the sidelines and listened attentively to her as she wove deceptive web.

"All right." He escorted her to the chairs at the seating area in the corridor. "Come with me. Wait here while I go speak with him." He continued down the hall to the office, knocked, and entered.

In the meantime, she peered at the paintings on the wall.

Leonard returned, "Mr. Kingsley will speak with you."

Tabitha turned to Uri, "Are you coming?"

"I'll stay here."

She shadowed Lenard on the way down the hall to the study, he opened the door and she entered the office.

16

Mr. Kingsley stood by the window near his desk holding a frame in his hand.

"Good afternoon, Mr. Kingsley," she said as she entered the room.

He made eye contact with her, "Good afternoon, Mrs. Ryan. Would you like a drink?"

"Yes, please."

He put the picture frame face-up on the desk.

"Have a seat." He walked over to the bar and put ice in a glass.

"Do you have any children, Mr. Kingsley?"

"Yes, I do. I have a son, but he left home a long time ago." He looked over his shoulder at her. "He wanted to spread his wings and start his own business, although he could've waited until I passed on to inherit my business."

"That's ambitious of him," Tabitha said. "At times, it's hard to accept but they choose their own path in life whether we like it or not."

"I'm aware of that, but he took it too far, went off and married a commoner." He brought the drink over to her and sat on the front of the desk.

"Anyway, let's get back on topic. What are you proposing, Mrs. Ryan?"

"I recently bought a hundred and forty-five acres on Draíocht Dol. The land is rich and perfect for planting crops."

"Why would I or anyone else for that matter want to acquire land there?" he asked.

"You're a resourceful man; I'm sure you can think of something, but I'll give you a few suggestions ... you can sow, harvest, and sell the crops in Vermouthshire."

"I'm already doing that here. You're wasting my time, Mrs. Ryan."

"Did your son start his business?" She put the glass to her mouth.

He sat there trying to figure her out. "I don't know where you're going with this but I'll bite." Mr. Kingsley sipped on his drink. "I haven't a clue. All I know is that he moved to one of the

153

other islands. I haven't heard from him since. *I warned him; I don't take kindly to competition*," the latter of his response mumbled under his breath.

Yet she heard him. "Was that your son in the photo earlier?"

"Yes." He reached for the frame, stared at it briefly and showed it to her.

Tabitha's heart sank as a knot formed in her throat when she realized who it was. "What's your son's name?"

"Albert Kingsley." He came to her in spirit and lied – gave her a fake last name but to be fair, imps weren't known for their honesty.

"When was the last you heard from your son?"

"Four years."

"I have a son too, but he recently passed away. Parents should cherish their children. You never know when you'll lose them," Tabitha said.

154

"I'm sorry for your loss. Forgive me but," Mr. Kingsley palmed his chin as he raised a brow. "I get the sense that you're here for another reason?"

"You're right. I'm Tabitha O'Brien."

The surname rang a bell. He cleared his throat. "And ...?"

She stood and began to pace the room. "Anton – your guard came to my residence and took my son's life. Not long afterward, he died in my arms, Mr. Kingsley." Her eyes filled with tears.

"I'm sorry—"

"Save your words," she cut him off. "... my son died because my husband refused to sell our crops to you." Her voice coarsened. "You're so used to having your way that when you couldn't, you revert to unsavory tactics," she raised her tone and charged at him, knocking him off the front of the desk onto his back.

"Look ... if its money you want, I have plenty of it." She knelt beside him and shoved her hand

155

to his neck, and commanded the rest of his body to stay still.

"I have no use for your money. I'll be leaving shortly, but before I go, I want you to know something."

"Lenard," he yelled.

With a sweeping gesture of her finger, she silenced him. Still standing in the hall, Uri heard a muffled voice coming from the study. He barged in and as he did so Tabitha's neck did a three hundred and sixty-degree turn and yet her hand remained at Kingsley's throat.

"Please—don't do it. Don't stoop to his level. It won't change anything."

"Don't interfere with affairs," she pointed at him. Uri stared at her with his heart beating tumultuously in his chest. He didn't approve of her actions but didn't dare to try and stop her. Meanwhile, Kingsley's eyes shifted frantically in his head.

"Now listen carefully ... your son, Albert is dead." Mr. Kingsley's eyes widened. "Yes." She smirked purely for satisfaction. "He's dead and he's probably been dead all along. I won't keep you much longer but I have one last question before I let you go. Did you send Anton to look for your son?"

Mr. Kingsley's head moved up and down.

Tabitha laughed. "One act of deviance, in turn, deserves another. He must have killed your son and his wife, Cora."

Mr. Kingsley's eyes stilled.

"Yes, I know them well." Her face stiffened as she placed the other hand around his windpipe and applied pressure until she shattered the bone after which blood flooded his windpipe. He lay there gurgling while he stared at her. Meanwhile, the veins in his eyes expanded, which ultimately spread like fractures within a thin sheet of glass, patiently observed as he drowned in his lifeblood.

"Thanks to you, I can't bury my loved ones. They were swept away by the wave and have yet to be found."

Tabitha coiled her fingers in an unnatural meandering motion directly above him just before the light went out of his eyes. Promptly, maggots occupied his body, eating their way through his core even as it ripened before her very eyes and swelled exponentially. Within a blink of an eye, his body exploded and at the same time, the pressure opened the door allowing Kingsley's remains to fly into the hallway. A pungent odor came with it that spread everywhere. Tabitha wiped his muck from around her eyes and flicked it off her hand, wiped her hands on her clothing. Uri wiped the bloody slush from his face with his sleeve, peeked inside, saw what was left of Mr. Kingsley and backed out.

Just then, a fire ignited in the room as Tabitha walked down the hall, passing Lenard on the way out with Uri close behind. They stood on the lawn and watched as the smoke quickly engulfed the hall.

"Fire!" Lenard shouted.

At that point, Mr. Newman burst through the double doors of the gallery and bolted down the hall to the study. By then, the entire room was overcome with flames. He peered through the flames. There wasn't anyone to save but Lenard swore that he saw Mr. Kingsley cowering in the corner.

"Please help me," Mr. Newman heard through the flames. It was his duty to protect him, so he had to think fast. He ripped one of the drapes from the hall window, covered himself with it, and charged into the room. Once Newman got past the flames, Lenard looked on, hoping that Newman would be successful, but he soon realized that his eyes had played tricks on him. By then, it was too late; the flames encircled him and burned through the drapes. Within a matter of seconds, Newman was on fire; his screams were so loud it traveled throughout the 12-room mansion. At the same time, the hallway filled with smoke, which made it difficult for Lenard to see. Therefore, he lowered himself to a crawling

159

position and crawled down the hallway with only the vague light from the front door to guide him, but that too faded. In no time, smoke filled his lungs causing him to lose consciousness. The fire raged on and spread throughout the entire mansion.

Only then did a sense of calm come over her as she witnessed the structure rapidly burning to the ground. Uri had no choice but to stand there quietly listening to the terrible screams and whimpers of the pending dead until they were completely silenced by her rage.

17

Eventually, the fire died; the fragments that remained left with the wind. As it did, grass grew in the place where the mansion once lied, leaving no clue of what was formerly there. Baffled by the horror, Uri stood awestruck of her powers.

"Let's go," she said and turned her back to that godforsaken place, hiked down Clod Hill, and ambled through the countryside's peaceful landscape to the downtown area. Hours later, they entered the town, met by people who stopped just to stare at their blood-soaked garments. Still, they kept their heads high and continued on their way even as the town folk held on to their children and spouses as they passed by the unofficial dignitaries of death.

Seeing the pier up ahead only hastened their steps and soon they approached their boat.

"Where will we go from here?" Uri asked as he helped her into the vessel.

"To Draíocht Dol." They left the port and sailed out to sea.

Rough seas kept them out there longer than usual, which only prolonged their arrival to Draíocht Dol, but halfway through the trip, the surf lessened. Shortly thereafter, the boat neared the pier giving them a view of the unrecognizable shoreline. The damaged port was a deterrent for the larger ships and nonresidents as a whole but the handful of shop owners rebuilding the stores was encouraging. Shortly afterward, they docked, got off the boat and approached a man sitting in the driver's seat of a parked wagon.

"You two all right?" the man asked as he got a good look at them.

"We're fine. Never mind our bloody rags," she said. "Can you take us inland?"

"Nothing's out there, but I'll take you if that's what you want."

"That might not be necessary. Do you have two horses that I can rent for a few hours?"

"Sure, I have two in a barn a half a mile from here."

"Can you take us there?"

"Sure." They got in the wagon and traveled down the dirt path to a barn not far away. Upon arrival, the driver brought the horses out and tied them to a post outside. Tabitha paid for their use, untied and mounted the horses.

"I'll have them back within three hours," she said as the horses trotted off.

They rode inland for about an hour, and along the way came upon their cabin. A few logs scattered around the yard were all that remained, but the majority of the structure was intact. Tabitha got off the horse and Uri followed suit. They saw a few stray dishes buried in the mud as they entered the cabin. They went outside together. Uri ventured out to the field and along the way, he kicked a rock that ricocheted off a white dome protruding from the dirt. He knelt down and brushed the dirt away.

"Did you find something?" she asked and walked up behind him.

"Yes."

She stooped down beside him to get a closer look. "It's a skull." She held the top and tugged it loose from the earth. Tabitha stared at the skull she had communicated with on countless occasions. Even after a flood, *he* emerged. She threw it; it hit a tree and on impact, it broke apart.

"There's someplace else I'd like to go before we leave Draíocht Dol. Let's go."

They mounted the horses; Tabitha led the way through high slopes and low valleys into the flatlands until they came upon a body of water.

"This is it." She stopped the horse, got down, and tied the horses.

"This is where we spent one of the happiest days of my life. Your father and I lay beneath this tree on a blanket while the horses grazed over there," her eyes gleaming as she spoke. She ambled to the pond ahead; Uri followed her. She looked down at her reflection rippling on the

164

surface of the water and wept. Initially, her tears went unnoticed but when Uri stood beside her, there was no hiding it.

"Your brother loved it here." She wiped tears. "He'd splash about this pond like a fish out of the water."

She peered at a rock nearby and noticed three turtles, two adult sized, and a smaller one resting there. Their decorative dark-green shells embellished with swirls of red and pale yellows brought a smile to her face knowing that even they had a sense of family. They looked about as content as the O'Brien's did when all was well.

Uri put his arm around her. "A beloved place such as this ought to have a special name. If given a poignant name it can potentially solidify its existence."

She sighed and looked around the landscape thinking of an appropriate name. "Turtle Pond seems appropriate. After all, it's their sanctuary now."